I0623487

LOVING LIV

GONE WILD #5

USA TODAY BESTSELLING AUTHOR
STACEY KENNEDY

This book is a work of fiction. Names, characters, places, and incidents are the product of the author's imagination or are used fictitiously. Any resemblance to actual events, locales, or persons, living or dead, is coincidental.

Copyright © 2020 by Stacey Kennedy. All rights reserved, including the right to reproduce, distribute, or transmit in any form or by any means. For information regarding subsidiary rights, please contact Stacey Kennedy.

Print Edition

Stacey Kennedy
www.staceykennedy.com

Edited by Lexi Smail
Copy Edited by Jolene Perry
Proofread by RaeChell Garrett
Cover Design by Jersey Girl Designs

Manufactured in Canada

For my dear readers who never gave up
asking for Miles's story…

PROLOGUE

THERE WERE SHORT men, tall men, and everything-in-between men. And then there was Miles Schantz, a man who stood out as *different*. Taller. Stronger. Sexier. Ruggedly handsome. Miles, the stranger who hailed from Las Vegas. His dark powerful eyes met Liv Sloane's while he sat at the table among his group of friends. He sipped his scotch, holding her stare like no one else mattered in the room but her. They were both in O'Keefe's Irish Pub tonight to celebrate the marriage of Gabe O'Keefe, the owner of the pub, and his new wife, McKenna. Liv only got an invite because Allie, her best friend and boss, was married to Micah Holt, a good friend of Gabe's. But while the outdoor ceremony at Crissy Field Park had been beautiful, with stunning views of the Golden Gate Bridge and San Francisco Bay, the reception at Gabe's pub was filled with delicious food and music from a live band. Liv had been transfixed by Miles all night. No matter how long she studied him, she couldn't quite put her finger on what made him so intoxicating.

"He's a Dominant."

Liv jerked her head toward her best friend. Allie looked beautiful most days with her long brown hair and big curls, but with shadowy makeup framing her blue eyes, she was stunning. She'd been dancing, leaving Liv at the bar to gawk at Miles. Liv hadn't realized she'd come back. "Pardon?"

Allie gestured at Miles, waggling her eyebrows. "You've been trying to figure out what's different about him, right? Well, that's what it is." She paused to take a quick sip of wine. "Actually, that's what is different about all of the men sitting at the table with him. They're all members of an exclusive sex club in Vegas, Club Sin. But keep that on the down low. I'm not supposed to know that, and neither are you."

"Sex club? Really?"

Allie nodded.

"Miles owns the nightclub that is the front for the secret sex club. It's called Club Sin."

"Interesting," Liv said, glancing back at Miles, who still watched her. The commanding nature in his gaze, the passion all but pulsating out of him...*a Dominant*. She guessed that made sense. He didn't smile or try to flirt, he *watched*. And something in the way he watched her made Liv's body take notice, her nipples puckering beneath her long cherry-colored dress with a slit in the front.

"Not like that should surprise you," Allie said, drawing Liv's gaze again. She gave a knowing look. "They are Micah's friends."

Liv acknowledged that with a nod. Allie owned a real estate company, and Liv was her assistant, so while they were on the job, they kept conversation strictly professional. Outside of work, she and Allie were extremely close, and from that friendship, Liv learned about a whole new world. One of Dominants and submissives and wild, erotic sex. A world that seemed a lightyear away from Liv's own shattered one. The reason for that was Gavin Humphries, a well-known playboy she'd given her heart to… the very boyfriend who proposed and then cheated. Two years had gone by since she'd broken things off, and she still wasn't over it. She hadn't dated, or even had sex, since. And the only orgasm she'd had lately was provided by her vibrator. She glanced back at Allie. "Do you know Miles well?"

"I know what's most important."

"Which is?"

Allie grinned. "He's single." She slid her arm through Liv's then her smile turned sly. "You've asked me before what it's like to be with a Dominant. Miles can't take his eyes off you. Girl, here's your chance. Take it!"

Liv considered just that, meeting Miles's gaze again. Her belly fluttered as he continued to watch her. Heady need overwhelmed her, warming her up in all the right places. Miles projected something richer than charm, this was seduction in its purest form. And he wasn't doing a damn thing. She turned back to Allie.

"Honestly, Allie, we both know I'm definitely not brave enough to make the first move."

Again, Allie grinned.

"Which is quite possibly your first lesson with a Dom. You don't make the first move."

Right then, a hand caressed her shoulder. Liv caught Allie's slight chuckle before Liv turned and stared into eyes that transfixed her. Suddenly, her heart was racing and butterflies filled her stomach.

"Can I have this dance?" Miles asked, his voice a low, deep rumble that hummed through her.

"Uh. Yes, sure," she breathed, sliding her hand in his. In that moment, something came over her. Something magical. Everything lit up inside her; slight nervousness matched with excitement.

He led her onto the dance floor and pulled her in close against the hard lines of his muscular body. He smelled like warm cinnamon and masculine leather and he felt like…*sin.* As she followed him in the dance, she caught his friends and their wives all watching her like she was a puzzle that amused them.

"Are you enjoying yourself tonight, Liv?"

His smooth voice felt like a heat wave washing over her as he guided her in the slow dance. "Very much so.

You?"

"Definitely," he murmured, his attention falling to her lips. "Now even more so."

Her breath caught somewhere in her throat as parts of her awakened that she thought were dead. Murdered by the crushing blow Gavin had delivered when he broke her heart. A reminder that had her looking a little more closely at Miles. A Dominant, he had to be a player. He must have women available to him at all times.

Miles's fingers tightened on her back, boldly holding her to him. "Allie told me you're single. I've been trying to figure out all night how that's possible."

I'm terrified to get hurt again. She laughed dryly. "Easy. I like being single. Don't you?"

His thumb brushed across hers and a jolt rolled through her. "Tonight, I'm very glad I'm single."

She *almost* snorted. Single. A nightclub. Dominant. Trouble. That's what this guy was. Pure trouble. The type of trouble that gathered hearts and threw them away. She nearly stepped away. She'd been here before and been burned. And yet...*and yet...*he was also the type of trouble that was perfect for a one-night stand. She could almost taste the friction between them. She felt more alive tonight than she had in years, desperate for a man's touch. *His* touch. She took a step forward, locked in this stranger's intensity, pulled by something she didn't want to control. "I am too," she said softly.

His eyes flared before he dropped his head and trailed his nose against her neck, making her shiver. Then he looked her right in the eye like he had nothing to hide. "We've got tonight, then?" he murmured.

"We've got tonight," she whispered.

His heated smile told her she wouldn't regret her choice.

And she didn't regret it. Not when they danced the night away. Not when he began kissing her. And certainly not when he pinned her to the brick wall in the alleyway after the groom and bride left for their honeymoon. Outside, the air moist, and the night dark, Miles's gaze skimmed over her parted lips, the move impossibly sexy, as she drew in a deep breath. A slight curve lifted his mouth as he grabbed a fist full of her ass and pressed his thigh between her legs. A whimper fell from her lips, and she found no shame in it.

His grin was pure sin. "I could have so much fun with you," he murmured.

Desperation filled her as she gripped his ripped biceps and ground herself against him. A low, very *male* sound came from deep in his chest. Suddenly, the scruff of his five o'clock shadow scraped against her cheek and down her neck as he placed a hot kiss there. His fingers tangled in her hair, pinning her like a promise she knew he could deliver on. And she wanted him to deliver. *Badly.* Gavin had stolen something from her when he cheated, not once, but five times over the course of their relationship. Tonight, with *this* man, she was going to get back her confidence.

Miles tightened his fingers, almost as if he knew her mind wandered. She shivered, and then his low chuckle brushed across her ear. "You're primed and ready, aren't you, Liv?" he murmured.

She moaned, not recognizing the need in her voice. "Yes," she rasped. "Don't wait."

And perhaps the same insane need drove him, too, since his mouth immediately dropped to hers and he kissed her in a way that no one ever had before. He tested and teased, giving her a kiss that had her nearly climbing his body to get closer. His pants were hastily pulled open, a condom quickly applied, and her panties were thrust aside. He nudged her legs open wider. She stood on her tip toes, melting into his kiss again, his tongue stroking hers, making her feel alive in ways she hadn't felt for so long. Wanted. Desired. All the things that had been stripped from her.

Then Miles was inside her, and her head fell back against the brick wall as a moan escaped her lips. She hadn't had a man touch her in so long, and every slow shift of his hips as he drove his hardened length inside her, only brought her higher. He was big. God, was he big, and the pleasure rippled through her.

But she didn't want slow.

"Harder," she said.

Miles nipped at her neck. "Such a bossy little thing."

She realized he might be turned off by her demands, but she couldn't help herself, and she felt the spread of his grin against her neck before he leaned away and set that potent stare on her. She wanted to lose herself in those piercing eyes and look away all at the same time. He penetrated places in her soul no one had ever touched, making her feel like he saw all the things everyone else missed. Her heart raced a little bit faster; her skin flushed a little bit hotter.

Before she could pull away, flee like she always did whenever someone got too close, he slammed forward, and her gasp echoed around her. "Stay right here with me, Liv," he murmured. "Don't run."

She shuddered against him. "I'm not running."

He brought his mouth close to hers and said softly, "You're blazing away from something, sweetheart." He gripped her hair tight, allowing her to feel every spectacular inch of him. Until he stopped. His lips brushed against hers. "I'm tempted to see how much more I can make this body shake." Only then did she realize he was right. Her legs were trembling. Hard. "But I'll give you what you need."

The conversation ended, and he kept the promise that his eyes had made earlier. His fingers never left her hair, his other hand held her ass as he fed her desire, driving into her, the misty air easing the burning of her cheeks, as he took her to a place she'd never gone.

One of total surrender.

Within his touch, and in this safe power he exuded, he claimed her body, and she allowed it, melting into him.

Until he stopped.

She cried out in frustration. So close, she was *right* there. Her entire body shaking now.

He slid both hands to her cheeks. Dark, addictive lust stared back at her. "One thrust and you'll shatter," he murmured. "Is that what you would like, Liv, to come?"

She tried to respond, but only another whimper came out.

Miles firmly held her gaze. "Tell me what you're running from, and I'll give you what you want."

"A broken heart," she managed.

At her answer he thrust once, with such force and intent, that she broke apart fast and hard, and somewhere in all of that, she heard him say, "Good girl."

CHAPTER 1

Three months later…

*W*HAT HAPPENS ON *the singles' cruise, stays on the singles' cruise.*

Liv smiled at the sign hanging behind the bar with a mix of amusement and horror. She had no idea how a vacation could go so wrong, so quickly, but there was no avoiding the shitshow that her old college friends had landed themselves in. They'd arranged the seven-day cruise to reconnect after years spent apart since graduation, except their planner, Kendall, had accidentally booked them on a singles' cruise instead of a relaxing one that Liv very much needed.

Standing on the main deck, Liv took in the pool. Barely-dressed people looked well past drunk at only seven o'clock at night, and a few couples were grinding against each other, eyes glossed over in pleasure. She couldn't stop the laughter from bubbling up. This trip would be a far cry from sunbathing with a book and sipping a fancy drink surrounded by lazy people wanting to do the same damn thing.

"I'm…I need to take a walk," said Kendall, her green eyes huge. She whirled, her brown hair flying around her before she took off like flames licked her feet.

Liv vaguely heard someone call Kendall's name, but she quickly took a step back as a drunk couple nearly knocked her over. They all but ate each other's faces and moaned sounds that apparently were totally appropriate on this cruise. *Dear Fate, what have you signed me up for now?*

Liv recalled being a bold woman three months ago, seeking lust instead of being the *good girl* that her parents raised her to become or the brokenhearted woman with ironclad guards. But that was then, and nothing exciting had happened since Miles had set off fireworks in her body.

Well, until this cruise.

She sipped her cocktail as the infectious loud laughter and music filled the deck. With Kendall, the 'mom' of the group, off sulking at mistakenly booking a singles' cruise, and her college best friend, Aubrey, a born wild child, off to God knows where, Liv turned to the more sensible ones of their group, Benjamin and Grace.

Mathematics professor, Dr. Benjamin Reed, took in the wild atmosphere with a smile. He had dark brown curly hair and clever brown eyes that always won men over. In truth, he probably needed this cruise in a big way, since he worked more than anyone she knew. And

Grace…well, Grace, with her buttoned up ways and tense brown eyes, needed an adventure. It occurred to Liv then that maybe Kendall didn't get it so wrong after all. And maybe…*just maybe*, the singles' cruise was exactly what they all needed.

Except for Liv. No, sir. Every single man ruined her life. Jonathan, her high school sweetheart, and the guy she gave her virginity to, picked up and left for college and never looked back. Then she suffered through first dates that were nearly torturous, only to have Allie introduce her to Gavin at work one day. She'd been as taken with him as every woman was. It seemed perfect, but really, that's when everything in her life went wrong. When Liv first got hired as Allie's assistant, her plan had been to work one year to get hands-on experience. Then she could get her real estate license and move into corporate real estate. At the time, Gavin had been—and still was—a big time corporate real estate agent. But she'd gotten so caught up in her relationship, that she never left her assistant position. Two months before their wedding, one of his mistresses showed up at their house. There were five mistresses in total, and it took Liv two years of therapy to put Gavin behind her. But even now, Liv knew she wasn't totally over what happened. One, she hadn't dated anyone since. Two, the annoying little voice in her head still told her, *"You weren't enough for him,"* every now and again. She'd sworn off men…until that night with Miles. While Miles never broke her heart, what he'd done was worse. He became unforgettable. His sizzling touch…those potent eyes watching her…that safe feeling he offered was in her head. All the damn time.

Case in point, as she sipped the final drops of her cocktail, tasting the tangy lime, she swore she saw him sitting on a stool at the other side of the bar. This had happened before. She saw Miles everywhere, all the time.

Until she blinked, and then she realized he wasn't there at all.

She sighed, turning away and placing her drink down on the shirtless waiter's tray as he walked by, while Benjamin and Grace chatted about the disaster of their ruined vacations. Liv didn't think it was a disaster. She was officially losing her mind and needed a break. Allie had a few deals closing this week, but Liv had left her in tiptop shape. Now she had seven days of fresh air and open waters, which was enough time to relax and think about what she needed to do to get her life back on track. Because lately, even Liv knew she wasn't just treading water, she was drowning. And being unable to forget the man who stripped her bare with one night together wasn't helping matters. The only thing she needed to do on this cruise was find that piece of her old self. The strong part that didn't obsess over men she couldn't have and certainly didn't want. Which was precisely why every time Miles called to come see her over the last few months, she came up with an excuse to keep him away. His life was in Vegas. Her life was in San Francisco. He was a Dominant. She was *not* looking to join a sex club. Thoughts of Miles, and wanting him, needed to end.

That was tough to do when she caught another glimpse of the Miles imposter across the bar. He hadn't disappeared. *Hmm.* She blinked. Twice. And yet…he remained. The laughter and splashing from the pool all disappeared under the weight of that gaze. The power of those eyes. Damn. This wasn't working at all.

With another deep sigh, she looked back at Grace and Ben, who still chatted, trying to ground herself. A quick look over her shoulder, and Miles still sat there. *Fuck.* The memory of him and his spectacular *everything* caressed her. She swore she could hear his voice and feel his touch, pulled in so deep she felt like the world simply slipped away. Goosebumps raced down her neck, need overwhelming her. She quickly cleared her throat, trying to shake off the feeling.

Determined to numb herself with booze, Liv interrupted Benjamin and Grace, "I'm going to get another drink. Want one?"

Both shook their heads, but Grace said, "I really want to get settled in my cabin."

"Go ahead," Liv replied. "I'll meet up with you later."

Benjamin winked. "Unless some hot guy grabs you first."

Liv pointed at him. "No men. I already told you. I'm done with your kind."

Benjamin laughed, and that warm sound she'd missed these past years followed her as she moved toward the other bar. She needed to get a closer look at the man who resembled Miles. She'd stay away from him for the next seven days, but she wanted to see him first. She didn't need a reminder of the guy she'd been trying so hard to forget. Really, it was silly. Most women would love the fact that they met a guy who made the molecules in their body explode, but Liv was not that woman. She'd already given her heart to a bad boy, and he'd given his body to any woman who would take him. And the truth was, Miles, and the way he captivated her, terrified her to her bones. That hurt, that strangling pain she'd endured with Gavin, she wouldn't put herself in that position again.

Not ever again.

She slowly drew closer to the man, and he never looked away. Heat rolled through her, puckering her nipples with every step, making warmth build between her thighs, just that easily, until she finally stood in front of him. She swore she could smell the hints of a warm leather in his cologne. But she'd experienced this before. Dozens of times over the last three months. She swore

Miles stood there in front of her, only to be mistaken. She lifted her hand and poked his chest, expecting the face to morph in a way that she didn't recognize, followed up by a "Sorry, do I know you?"

That's not what happened.

Miles arched a single eyebrow at her. "Interesting way to say hello."

"Shit." She yanked her hand away. "You're real." She shook her head, taking another full step back, blinking rapidly. "I mean, it's *you*."

Miles chuckled. "Were you expecting it not to be?"

She blinked. Twice more. It had been three months since she'd seen him, but he looked exactly the same. Her cheeks flushed at being reunited with the guy she'd blatantly rejected every single time he called to try and come see her in San Francisco. Sure, they weren't her finest moments, but she didn't trust herself with this guy. At all. "How did you…what is…*why* are you on this cruise?"

Something crossed his face, maybe confusion. "You didn't know I was coming?"

She paused, her thoughts reeling. "Should I have known?"

He nodded and frowned. "Two weeks ago, I got an email from you telling me that you wanted me to join you on this cruise." He angled his head, those intense eyes boring into hers. "I guess it's right to assume you never sent the email."

Liv's mouth dried, the ground falling out from beneath her. "Someone sent you an email inviting you here?"

"Yes, they did," he said with a slow nod. "And I thought that someone was you."

Liv racked her brain, trying to understand who would do that. But then it all made sense, and Aubrey was the most likely candidate. Aubrey...who had so conveniently disappeared when they all decided to come to the pool bar. Her best friend from college knew *all* about Miles. "Those busybodies, meddling—"

"Friends from college that you're here with," Miles offered, obviously aware of who she came with on the cruise.

Liv gave a firm nod. "Friends that I plan to murder."

Miles laughed, a low rumble that made Liv's heart skip. "I really don't think that's a good idea. You're too gorgeous to go to jail. They'd eat you alive."

Heat licked through her at the compliment. "I..."—she cleared her throat—"I need to go get settled into my cabin." She looked over her shoulder, finding Grace and Benjamin heading toward the glass elevators. "My friends, they're leaving."

"Before you run off, we need to discuss our current predicament."

His confident, deep, seductive voice lured her back

to him, and she gulped at the intensity in which he watched her. Like he was a lion, and she was his toy. "What's to discuss?"

He held her gaze. "If your meddling friends were right and you wanted to see me again? Or if I should get off this ship?"

Those traitors. Whoever did this, whatever game they were playing, someone was going to pay. She'd told them all about how she was seeing Miles everywhere after their hot night together. And then she told Aubrey how life felt dull since that night. Still! No one had the right to make this decision for her. She fought to pull together her thoughts. "No…yes…I…"

His eyebrows slowly drew together at her stumbling. "It's yes or no, Liv. Either you want me to leave this ship or you want me to find another wall to fuck you against." His grin dripped sex.

Sweet Jesus.

She parted her lips to tell him to leave. That this was a *huge* misunderstanding. That it could never work between them, and she wouldn't repeat her mistakes. But she was pulled in by the heat he exuded. Months she'd thought of him, *needed* him again. She didn't want him to leave. She wanted him closer.

The entire cruise ship began to vanish as Miles closed the distance between them. He didn't touch her. Oh, hell no, he dropped his head into her neck, drawing in her scent like he'd been craving it, and now that he'd gotten his fill, all was right with the world again. When he finally leaned away, one look into those eyes, that heated promise, and her knees went weak.

He took his time looking at her parted lips before meeting her eyes. "I'm glad to see you again, Liv," he finally murmured. A hard shudder ran through her as he dropped a single kiss to her cheek. Her eyes fluttered shut, and the memory of his touch sent need straight between her thighs, making her wet and desperate. When he leaned away, he gave her that panty-dropping grin— like he'd gotten the answer to whatever question he had. "I think I'll stick around. Something tells me it's going to get interesting."

As he walked away, she could finally talk again. "Yeah, that's what I'm afraid of."

CHAPTER 2

M ILES ENTERED HIS luxury cabin at the back of the ship, undecided if he should laugh at the situation or dive into the ocean and swim back to shore. For two weeks, he'd been clamoring to see Liv again. Their night together had shifted something inside him, opened his eyes to new possibilities, making him realize how small his world had been. Meanwhile, Liv was hellbent on killing whoever had tricked them into reconnecting on this trip. To be honest, Miles was right there with her. He slammed the door behind him, taking in the sheer size of the suite. He never usually spent money like this on himself, but he had planned for Liv to spend the trip with him in this room and he had wanted the space, and the balcony. His gaze shifted there, the white curtains dancing in the wind with the warm breeze. He had plans for that balcony, which included bending Liv over the railing and taking them both where they wanted to go.

He cursed, frustrated that wasn't happening, and he kicked off his shoes, ready to figure out his next steps.

The last thing he wanted to do was make a wrong move now. Since their night together, Miles had tried to fly out to San Francisco to see Liv again. She'd shut him down every damn time. Even though he finally gave up texting her after all of her excuses, not a day had gone by that she wasn't on his mind. Hell, she was there in the blood in his veins. A hunger he couldn't could quench. And none of it made any sense. Miles liked freedom. He loved women even more, specifically submissive women. Liv was pure vanilla, with guards up around her heart that made it impossible to get anywhere near her. He liked his women open emotionally and sexually free, and she was neither. She was all wrong for him, and yet, he couldn't get her out of his damn head. Enough so, that when the email came inviting him on the cruise, he didn't think twice about joining her.

The balcony drew him out, but as he grabbed a beer from his fridge, his phone rang. He reached for his cell in his pocket and snorted at the screen. Preparing himself for the storm facing him, he stepped out onto the balcony and dropped into the lounge chair. Off in the distance, he spotted the twinkling of lights on land, precisely why he'd booked this cabin. The position on the back of the ship offered a one-eighty-degree view over the stern's wake. "Hello, ladies," he answered the Facetime call.

Four beautiful faces were squished together. Cora,

Presley, Kenzie, and Ella, the wives of his closest friends, and fellow Dominants who belonged to the exclusive Las Vegas BDSM dungeon, Club Sin.

Cora's bright blue eyes sparkled. "Tell us everything that's happened," she said.

"Don't leave anything out," the strawberry blonde, Kenzie, added.

By the red velvet fabric behind them, Miles knew they were sitting on the big circular chair that rested in the middle of Club Sin. The lack of noise, both music and screams of pleasure, told him that the club was either between scenes, or the night hadn't begun yet. Miles hadn't looked at the clock since he'd gone onto the deck in search of Liv. "I've got very little to tell you," he answered them honestly. "Liv had no idea I was coming here."

"What?" Ella gasped, her long hair was swept to the side in a braid. "How is that possible? I thought Liv sent you the email."

"You and me both," Miles grumbled.

Presley's emerald colored eyes softened as she twirled a dark blond ringlet around her finger. "Do you have any idea who did send the email?"

"No, but I plan to find out." He looked like a damn idiot chasing a woman on a cruise who didn't want him there. Someone needed to answer for that. The only reason he wasn't jumping ship and hunting that person down was because Liv hadn't told him to leave. Just being near her again sparked that burning passion between them, making absolutely no sense. Miles knew lust. The pull he had to Liv, a woman he'd only touched once, exceeded lust. She was as alluring as she was the night he'd met her. He wanted *her*. Her innocence didn't push him away like it had with any other woman. Her guards didn't make him flee. He'd called every few weeks to see her, knowing she'd likely shut him down. Liv was *different*. He'd only wanted to understand why, and regardless of how he'd gotten here, he'd take the chance fate had given him.

Kenzie, always the loudest one of the bunch, asked, "Well, what are you going to do now? You're not going to leave, right? You're still going to go after her?"

They wanted gossip. Now their lives were filled with babies and playdates and routines, and for the last couple weeks, Miles' love life had become their entire focus. Not that he'd indulged them. "A Dom never tells his secrets, ladies. You should really know this by now."

Pouts followed.

"Harassing Master Miles *again*," Dimitri said firmly, yet his voice was tinged with amusement. Club Sin had been Dmitri's brainchild, and he only handed over the reins to Miles when he realized he couldn't have it all. The club. The family. And be the CEO of one of Las Vegas's top casinos. "Now, ladies, don't you have anything better to do? Or shall I give you something to do?" All sets of eyes flicked up at Dmitri and the women promptly cringed.

Miles smiled as they shot up from their seats, the phone moving until Cora's face showed on the screen. "Don't be your easygoing self about this. You deserve happiness. Don't leave that ship without her."

He didn't give Cora the confirmation she was looking for, but he acknowledged her affection with a soft nod. "Be well, Cora." All four women were kind and sweet, and also, incredibly nosy when they wanted to be.

The phone jiggled some more until Dmitri's sharp blue eyes regarded Miles. His longtime friend smiled warmly. "They are determined to make sure this works out for you."

"I was determined to make sure this works out for me, too, until I found out she didn't want me here," Miles admitted.

Dmitri frowned. "Obviously, someone thought she wanted you there, or why would they have sent that email? Seems to me Liv isn't being honest about not wanting to see you. Maybe she needed a push, and that email was it."

Miles had considered the same thought. "Possibly."

"Did she tell you to leave?"

"No," Miles said. "But she also didn't tell me to stay either." He ran a hand over his face. "I've never in my life met a woman who melts when I get close, and at the same time, does not want to see me."

Dmitri chuckled. "Women are complicated creatures. Passion can't be faked. There's a reason she's trying so hard to keep you out. Find out what that reason is, and I bet you'll find the answer you're looking for."

Miles gave a slow nod. "Thank you, Dmitri."

"Of course. Let us know if you need anything."

The phone shook again, and muffled voices filled the line, obviously Dmitri catching up the others.

Then Kyler was grinning at him. A cop, and a royal pain in Miles's ass on most days. "How's that vanilla treat of yours?" Kyler asked, his messy brown hair falling over his brow.

"As vanilla as ever." Miles smiled. Which, in truth, was still a shock to him. Miles *never* had vanilla sex. Sure, taking Liv outdoors in a back alleyway at the wedding wasn't exactly boring sex, but it was as vanilla as Miles had gotten since he'd turned twenty-one. He got off on erotic play, but touching Liv felt very similar. The high was just the same.

Nothing looked the same after their night together. Everything shifted. Club Sin lost its flavor. Running the nightclub lacked its usual excitement. Miles felt restless and bored, not the right state for any Dominant. But his biggest problem? He hadn't had sex with a single woman since Liv, no matter how many willing submissives crossed his path. Sure, he'd done scenes with submissives for demonstrations and when a submissive requested him personally, but he'd used toys in the scene, never himself. And there lay his problem. He needed to either make a go with Liv or put his curious interest in her to bed and make the changes necessary in his life to bring that excitement back.

The phone shuffled around again, and Porter, a private investigator, suddenly appeared on the phone, standing behind Kyler. "What's the plan now?"

Miles took a long sip of his beer and glanced out at the dark, rippling water, considering. The odd thing about Liv was that he understood she was running. Once she told him she'd had a heartbreak, he'd felt this odd tug to understand her past. Emotions had never been his thing, but when he touched Liv, his entire soul changed, fully in tune with her. He needed to explore that, understand why this vanilla woman had him all caught up. "The plan is simple. Remind her of this wild fucking thing between us. And now that we're on a cruise ship, and she's got nowhere to run, I can work on those guards she's got up."

"That simple?" Kyler grinned.

Miles nodded. "That simple."

"Nothing is ever that simple," Dmitri said, off in the distance.

Miles acknowledged his remark with another nod,

knowing that was true. For three months, he'd wanted to see Liv to no avail. But that thought only reinforced his decision now. He'd seen the desire in her eyes tonight. She was worth the fight and the hits to his ego. "Porter, can you do me a favor and find out who sent me that email?"

"Consider it done," Porter said. "I'll text details when I have them."

"Thank you," Miles said.

The phone shifted again.

Dark-haired Aidan took the phone next. "Listen, I'm not sure who would be stupid enough to trick you like this, but Cora had it right. This one, she's different. You're different with her. Don't leave that ship without her."

These men were his friends. They'd had many years of friendship between them and understood him the way only another Dominant would. Together, as Masters of Club Sin, they had built a fine establishment with a flawless reputation. But something was missing. In the last year, Miles had sold his construction company in a multi-million-dollar deal in order to oversee Club Sin. But what he hoped he'd find in the nightclub—the personal life he'd been missing—he hadn't found. His six closest buddies were married, settled with children. Miles's life had stalled. He needed change. And no matter what happened with Liv on the ship, change would come after the cruise ended. "Now if you're all done sticking your noses into my business, can I go and see about getting myself this woman?"

"Wait…" Cora called and then gasped.

Kyler appeared laughing. He looked into the phone and winked. "Cora had something to say, but she's currently indisposed."

"I'm sure she is," Miles said, imagining exactly what her Master made her mouth busy with.

Dmitri took the phone again. "You'll keep in touch?"

"I will."

"Enjoy yourself, all right?"

"I'll do that too." And just before the screen went dead, Cora's scream of pleasure echoed across the phone line.

Miles smiled and dropped his head back on his lounger, staring out at the dark, open waters, the moon glistening down on the ocean. He felt torn between his life at Club Sin, and this empty feeling in his chest that had come after his night with Liv. As he chugged back the cold, hoppy lager, and the laugher drifted up from the deck below, that emptiness eased slightly. Liv was close, and even though she hadn't sent that email, someone who loved her had. Even Miles sensed there was magic still between them. He wasn't ready to walk away from that just yet. The good thing was, he had six days to test the waters and find out why someone wanted them on this cruise ship together.

CHAPTER 3

L IV HAD NEVER understood insomnia, until this morning. Everything felt tired, from her heavy eyelids to her feet dragging against the wood floors as she strode across the pool deck. Miles was somewhere on this ship, and every part of her wanted to go and find him. Except her heart. And last night, her heart won. There were a hundred reasons why she and Miles couldn't work out. Exactly why she'd turned him down every time he called with an offer to visit or fly her out to him. At first, turning him down was easy, but even she'd gotten bored of her excuses. And the very worst part was when he'd stopped calling. When that happened, she couldn't help but talk about him to her friends. Obviously, those conversations had been enough reasoning for whoever arranged to have him come on this cruise. Deep down, Liv knew why one of her friends had done this. She hadn't been herself after Miles. She felt lonelier now than she had after Gavin, and that made no sense. She'd spent years with Gavin and a single night with Miles. But Miles reminded her what a man felt like. How being wanted and desired made her feel, and lately, she realized, she felt like she'd been asleep. Miles woke her up. And maybe she'd been a little too vocal about that fact, and this intervention was a well-meaning friend trying to fix a wrong.

Liv moved across the deck that had been full of partygoers last night. At eight o'clock this morning, the place was empty, and for this one second, Liv took it all in, trying to piece together this odd twist in her vacation.

Miles.

He'd come all this way, spent all this money, just because of one email from her. Of course, she felt flattered. But she'd already played out this scenario, and as much as she wanted Miles, the thought of it strangled her. With Gavin, she'd known loving him would cost her from day one. He was the playboy, the charmer, the guy every girl wanted. And regardless of the risk, she'd dove in headfirst, believing that she had just been the lucky one. It shouldn't have surprised her that a man good with the ladies, with enough confidence to make him stand out, would cheat, and yet it had shaken her entire world. He'd crushed her and then left her. She'd promised herself that, in order to date anyone again, everything had to make sense. And living in two different states most definitely didn't make sense.

Besides, Miles was also not the nice, respectable, polite man she should take home to her parents. Hell, no, he was the guy who ripped your clothes off then asked for your name later. Trouble, with a capital T, looking for a woman to play out all his erotic sexual fantasies. Liv was not that woman. Not even close to that woman. There was reason after reason to not let anything happen between them. She couldn't ignore those reasons; the pain sitting raw in the center of her chest wouldn't let her.

She finally made it to the balcony and she realized she could no longer see the horizon, only the gorgeous sun glistening against water.

"You better have a good reason for getting us up so early," Benjamin said behind her.

Liv whirled around to her so-called friends. Even with her anger, warmth touched her. These had been her people through college. Real friends that had been there every day, and each and every one of them brought something special to Liv's life. She'd missed them all, and being near them brought happy memories.

Liv noticed Kendall seemed put back together. "You're looking far better than you did the last time I saw you," Liv pointed out.

Kendall waved her off and yawned behind her hand. "Sleep can do amazing things."

Yeah, right. Only two things made Kendall have that calm, in control look, and those were having a plan of action and sex. Considering she was the reason for the singles' cruise debacle, Liv wondered if Kendall had gotten the latter last night.

She immediately shook the thought from her mind. *Who* or *what* Kendall did was not the current problem.

Before Liv could get to murdering someone, Grace dropped down onto the patio chair, stretched out her legs, and wiggled her pencil skirt down as low as possible to her knees. "Can I just point out that while everyone is always harping on me for working too much, I'm not the one who made us get up early."

Liv blinked in surprise at Grace's bare legs. She always wore pants. "You're wearing a skirt," she commented before she could stop herself.

"Yes." Grace glared. "I know."

Aubrey flicked her long blond hair over her shoulder and smiled. "And look at those fine legs. Gorgeous!"

Grace sighed, tugging on the hem of the skirt again. "Please, let's talk about anything other than my legs."

Right. Liv drew in a sharp breath, getting them back to the reason she'd called them here this morning. "I know it's early, and I'm sorry, but it's important," she explained to her current frenemies with a glare. "Which one of you brought Miles here?"

Every set of eyebrows shot up.

It came as no surprise that Aubrey spoke first. "What are you talking about?" she asked, her brown eyes narrowed as she folded her arms.

Through college, Liv was close to Benjamin, Grace and Kendall, but she and Aubrey were just a little closer since they'd been roommates. Liv widened her stance and placed her hands on her hips. "One of you sent an email to Miles, pretending to be me, and told him that I wanted him to come on the cruise. So, fess up, who did it?"

"Wait," Grace said slowly, sliding her legs off the chair and pulling on the skirt again. "That guy you were taking to yesterday on the pool deck…that was Miles? Like, *the Miles* who rocked your world apart?"

Liv gave a firm nod. "Yes, *that* Miles."

Benjamin whistled, shaking his head slowly. "Well, now I see what the fuss is all about. That man is a gorgeous specimen."

"Him being gorgeous is beside the point," Liv argued, feeling the burn in her cheeks. Sure, Miles was hot. So damn hot that the world had drifted away when his eyes caught hers, but still… "Which one of you did it? Tell me now, and if you've got a good enough reason, then I'll forgive you." Not before she got violent, of course.

"Wasn't me," they said in unison.

"How can I believe that?" Liv demanded. "Who else would do this?"

Every single person shrugged.

Liv scanned their faces, one by one, looking for any

signs they were lying. They all had one tell that Liv had learned through the years of friendship. Aubrey usually smiled. Benjamin avoided eye contact. Grace nibbled her lip. And Kendall could never stand still. But there was none of that now, every expression resembled sheer confusion, probably looking much like Liv had when she realized Miles wasn't a figment of her imagination. "This is so, so bad," Liv finally grumbled, plopping onto the chair closest to her and cupping her hands over her face.

"Oh, please," Aubrey clipped. "The guy who gave you the best sex of your life is here and probably wants to give you more sex. How is this bad?"

Liv slowly lowered her head. "You know why. For me…" She hesitated, not even wanting to say it.

Grace said softly, "You're tending to that battered heart, and he's a risk."

Grace always seemed to understand. "Exactly," Liv said with a nod. "I already told you all. I came here to forget him. To get past this…*moment*…and like some sick joke he's actually here."

Benjamin cocked his head. "Well, it's obviously clear that someone thinks he should be. Who else have you told about him?"

Liv racked her brain. "Just Allie at home," she eventually said. "But she would never do this to me." Though she planned to ask Allie, of course, but Allie was beyond loyal, and she knew how messed up Liv had been over

Miles.

Grace asked, "Well, did you tell him to leave?"

Liv knew the reaction she was going to get. "No."

Slow smiles greeted her.

"Stop it. Seriously, this is terrible. I'm not supposed to want him, remember? He's all wrong for me."

Aubrey gave Liv a knowing look. "I'm not seeing how this is a bad thing? You told us that you've been feeling all messed up about him, and that you wish you lived closer to make a go out of it. Why don't you use this as your chance to actually see if there's something more between you than sex?"

Grace agreed with a nod. "It makes sense. Maybe you've just hyped him up in your mind or something, but spend six days with him, and maybe this magical man you've created won't be so magical in the end."

"Maybe," Liv agreed.

Benjamin smiled. "And if things don't work out, at least you spent six days having amazing sex."

Liv laughed. "I suppose that is true."

Aubrey smiled. "Regardless of what you do or what happens, babe, we're here for you."

"Thanks," Liv said, feeling a whole lot better. "Before I even figure out what to do, I still have to accept this is all happening."

A couple walked by, hand-in-hand. Kendall followed them with her gaze then glanced back, crossing her arms.

"Oh shit, what if he's a stalker? We can't leave her with a stalker. What kind of friends would we be?"

The thought had crossed Liv's mind too. "Okay, let's consider that, though. Why would he pay money to come on a cruise? I mean, if he was going to stalk me, wouldn't he just do that in San Fran for the price of a cheap hotel?"

"Haven't you seen the news lately," Kendall countered. "People kill people on cruise ships all the time. I heard about this husband who killed his wife, and all of his family was on the cruise, children included."

"Kendall," Grace said, rolling her eyes. "I doubt he's come to kill Liv."

"I'm just saying, you never know." Kendall shrugged.

Liv considered it for a good few seconds and then shook her head. "I really don't get the killer vibe from him."

"Um, hello, have you seen Ted Bundy?" Kendall pointed out.

"Stop scaring her," Aubrey said with a frown at Kendall. "Let's come back to reality. Obviously, he's got these same feelings you have. You said it yourself that he's been calling for like three months trying to come out to see you. There's something between you two. Maybe you should explore that."

"I agree completely. Let's explore that."

Liv expelled a breath at Miles's low, smooth voice.

She kept her attention on her friends, who all smiled at Miles. Benjamin was giving him a very thorough once over with appreciation in his eyes. He had a taste for the bad boys too. That was one thing they always had in common.

"I take it you're the college friends," Miles said to her group.

"We are, but none of us are the ones who sent the email," Benjamin said. He offered his hand. "I'm Benjamin. This is Grace, Kendall, and Aubrey."

Miles returned Benjamin's handshake then smiled at the others. "Nice to meet you."

Kendall took Grace's hand, yanking her up from her chair. "Likewise, and we're also the friends who are leaving."

"Wait—" Liv called, as they all booked it toward the door.

Except for Aubrey. Her fiery, blonde spitfire of a friend closed the distance between her and Miles and narrowed her eyes. "Are you here to hurt Liv?" she asked, in a strong voice that didn't match her warm appearance.

Miles didn't even hesitate. He grinned, devilishly. "Only if she asks me too." He paused to wink. "And even then, I suspect she'd like it."

Aubrey's eyes went huge and her mouth fell open before she collected herself, pointing at Miles like her finger was a knife. "Let's be perfectly clear. I know who you are, and if you're here because you're stalking her, I suggest you go home at the next port, or you'll regret it." She stomped over to Liv and kissed her cheek. "We'll see you at breakfast in a few?"

Liv nodded. "You will."

"And don't forget our group massages and poolside piña coladas later," she added, marching her way over to the others.

Miles's low chuckle broke the silence. "I do not want to cross her."

"You really don't," Liv said, and slowly rose. "Aubrey is a force of nature."

He watched every single move she made until she stood in front of him, beneath his powerful stare. "They love you."

She nodded and smiled. "They do, and I love them."

He watched her for a long moment with questions simmering in his eyes. "Did you find out who the culprit of email fraud was?"

"Sadly, no," she said with a sigh. "You?"

"Not yet," he said. "But I've got a friend investigating it for me."

"Good," she replied.

A beat.

Miles stepped closer, and Liv, reflexively, stepped back, only realizing she did so when her back bumped against the railing. He placed his hands on either side of her, leaving no space between them, and leaned in, infusing the air with his warm, leathery aroma. "Let's get everything out in the open, all right?"

"Get what out in the open?" *Dear God, where had the air gone?*

He stared at her mouth, licking his lips before looking into her eyes again. "The fact that someone set this up to get us together again, leads me to believe you've been thinking about me. Have you?" he asked.

No. That should have been her answer, and yet that's not what came out of her mouth. "I…it's…complicated."

"It cannot be that complicated." The strength of his body right *there,* the heat, engulfed her.

For the first time in three months, she didn't feel uneasy. She felt like she was right back in that moment when he'd taken her outside in the alleyway, where she felt alive. "But it is," she rasped, wanting those sizzling lips back on hers like they had been that night.

She forced her attention back to his eyes when he said, "Then let me uncomplicate it. Tell me to go, Liv. Tell me you haven't been thinking about me. Tell me you don't want me here to explore this insane chemistry we've got, and I'll go home at the next port. It's that simple."

Why was her mouth not opening and saying the words? *Yes, go! We cannot make this work. I don't want complicated. And you're complicated.*

She parted her lips and then shut them before she forced the words from her mouth. "What if I don't tell you to go, but staying would be a really bad idea?"

A slow, dangerous smile stretched across his face. He dropped his mouth so close to hers, only a hairsbreadth away, teasing her with the spectacular kiss he could give her. "I suppose I would say I hope you enjoy your morning, Liv," he finally said. "And I'll be seeing you again soon."

With that hot promise back in his eyes, he strode off, and the air returned. Liv collapsed back onto a chair, her body in flames. She wanted him. Naked. Now.

"Miss, can I get you something?"

Liv looked up, shielding her eyes from the sun, finding a waiter. "Tequila."

His brows went up. It was only eight-thirty in the morning.

"Tequila," she repeated, dropping her hand onto her stomach full of butterflies. "The biggest shot you can find."

CHAPTER 4

L ATER THAT AFTERNOON, Miles waited by the bar. The day had been long and irritating and he'd spent the majority of his morning in the gym burning off adrenaline. He'd chased Liv onto this cruise, but that's where his chasing stopped. The last thing he wanted to do was scare her off, especially since her friends already suspected him of being a stalker. He'd spent an hour on the treadmill running off his ego. So far, he'd been made to look like an idiot and a fool. And yet, he knew Liv would come find him, just as much he knew he'd stay on this cruise no matter how many shots were thrown his way. Some unknown force pulled them together. Something that had him take her in the alleyway at his friend's wedding like some horny teenager who couldn't control himself.

Miles practiced control. He never lost it. Until *her*.

That had to mean something. But it was pretty damn clear that Liv was running from her past. Someone had carelessly handled her and her emotions, and nothing irritated Miles more. He wanted her heart open, free to explore, not to shut down every time he got close. Their night had proven to him that one thing could get past those guards she'd erected. His touch.

He took a swig of his crisp, cold larger, when suddenly the noise from the partygoers went silent. The crowd faded away as the gorgeous, guarded woman walked onto the deck of the ship. At the wedding, Liv had been dressed in a sexy red dress and high heels that had made her legs nearly delectable. When he saw her yesterday, she'd dressed for comfort, wearing capri leggings and a tank top. Now she wore ripped jean shorts and a white lacy tank top. Her hair was straight and down, and he liked this look best on her. Well, that was partly true. He suspected he'd like her naked best, but seeing her being herself was nice too. She scanned the crowd, stopping when her big brown eyes found him. The soft smile curving her mouth had him smiling back. Nothing made him happier than knowing his instincts were right. It cemented his plan.

He noted her long, deep inhale before she beelined for the bar. He chuckled, not minding her nerves. In fact, he loved that shy innocence. It tempted him to play with it a little. He pondered his next move, took in the area, and found a crowd around the tiki hut off to the side of the pool. A quick listen to the announcer on the microphone and the hooting and hollering made his smile widen. One touch…that's all he needed to get her to see this thing between them was greater than lust, and heat built in his groin at the anticipation of feeling her soft skin beneath his hands.

Liv remained at the bar, waiting to order up a drink, as Miles hopped off and went toward the tiki hut. He grabbed a fifty from his wallet and maneuvered toward the crowd.

"All right, beautiful ladies, who's next?" a young man called with golden skin and whiskey-colored eyes. His name tag read: Alfonzo.

Miles held his fifty up, and Alfonzo's gaze immediately locked onto the bill before he moved in Miles's direction. "See that brunette in the white tank top and ripped jean shorts by the bar," Miles explained, as Alfonzo covered his microphone with his hand. "Her name is Liv Sloane. Get her on your bar and there's another fifty in it for you."

The guy stared at Liv across the way and grinned from ear-to-ear. "Consider it done." He raised the microphone again. "All right, my beautiful people, let's see, who should we bring up next?" Even though women bounced, hands raised in the air, Alfonzo headed out of the tiki hut and moved straight to Liv. "Miss. You. Liv Sloane."

Liv slowly turned around; her eyebrows raised. She had a small straw in her mouth as she drank her fruity cocktail.

Alfonzo added, "It's body shot time."

Liv choked on her drink and began shaking her head, adamantly. She took a quick look around, and Miles bet she was looking to see if her friends were around. Which they weren't.

She backed away, but Alfonzo took her hand and pulled. "Come, Miss Liv, it's your turn."

Her mouth moved and she pulled against his hand.

"Liv. Liv. Liv," Alfonzo chanted into the microphone.

The crowd in the pool area joined in, yelling loudly, until every person on deck was yelling Liv's name.

Miles couldn't fight his smile, leaning a shoulder against the tiki hut and crossing his arms. He hoped his plan wouldn't backfire and end with her throwing a drink in his face. But somehow, he trusted his own judgment. She might not like this push at first, but he'd bet money that Liv, while innocent, wanted an adventure.

Liv glanced around at everyone chanting her name and visibly sighed, her shoulders lowering. She set her drink down at the bar and waved Alfonzo on, defeat in her eyes. Then those eyes narrowed on Miles as she walked toward him. "Was this your doing or is my traitor at it again?"

Miles slowly lifted an eyebrow. "Does it matter?"

Alfonzo tugged her along before she could answer,

and he heard her curse.

Miles laughed as she looked miserable climbing onto the bar, while the crowd continued chanting her name. When she lay back, her knees bent, Miles took the other fifty-dollar bill from his hand and gave it to Alfonzo, who backed away, still chanting Liv's name.

Miles stepped forward then, slowly, intently. He'd done many great things with a crowd watching. He enjoyed having eyes on him, the way it felt, like he controlled the world. How people studied the way he moved, how he dealt with a woman, and the way he could make her body react. Most of all, the way he could make her scream. Fuck yeah, he loved that.

"I'm going to kill you," Liv said as Miles sidled in next to her.

He studied her. Every fucking beautiful inch laid out for him, until he reached her eyes. There, he found her face flushed for another reason. Her pupils dilated with red-hot lust, begging him to burn hotter. He slowly shook his head and grinned. "No, Liv, you won't." The arousal in her face only deepened. He leaned down and said just to her in her ear, "You'll want to fuck me."

He heard her slight whimper. When he straightened, her chest rose and fell with deep breaths, as those gorgeous eyes pulled him. Christ, he could all but smell her desire seeping into the air, and he hadn't even touched her yet. This was what had stayed on his mind for the last three months, the very reason he kept trying to see her. She simply reacted to him being close. And damn, did he react, too, his cock hardened to steel, his mouth watered to taste her. And that same pulsating energy fed him as he nudged her leg with the tips of his fingers. One, then the other until she straightened out her legs for him.

"Your shot of Tequila," Alfonzo said behind Miles.

"Thank you." Miles took the shot and placed it next to Liv's shoulder. When he put his attention back on Liv, she stared at him directly. He noted the hitch of her breathing and had no doubt if he placed his fingers against her pulse, her heartrate would be hammering.

Aware of the crowd, and not giving a shit about them, he slid his gaze down her body, giving her the attention she deserved. He tucked his finger beneath the hem of her tank top, and flicked his attention to her face when she gave him a sweet tremble. Damn was he tempted to simply steal her away and give them what they both wanted. Instead, he grinned a promise that he'd increase that tremble if she let him. She nibbled her lip, those dark, hooded eyes on him. He held her eye contact, and as slowly as he could manage, nudged her tank top up, dragging his fingers across her warm flesh. She trembled again when he reached the bottom of her bra and tucked her shirt there.

He knew this body, and when he grabbed her jean

shorts on either side and pulled her forward so her legs dangled off the side, he was not surprised when she gasped. Her hands came down on his forearms, holding tight, the flush on her cheeks darkening. She liked a dominant touch. That he remembered vividly. Wanting to give her all she needed and more, he stepped between her thighs, nudging them aside as he did so, and the crowd went wild.

Her breathing was ragged, her stomach perfect, and her lips parted begging for his kiss. Her fingernails dug into him as he leaned over her and used the flat of his tongue to drag a line down her belly, stopping to swirl around her belly button and continuing on until he gave a slow flick at the top of her jean shorts, teasing her with what he could do on her clit.

The shiver she gave only made him draw this out slower. Teasing her, tempting her, with what the next six days and nights could bring. He grabbed the salt next to him and sprinkled it along the line of his saliva on her belly. She practically panted now as he took a cut-up lemon off the tray and placed it at the base of her throat.

She moaned when he poured the shot into her belly button, letting it spill over her stomach. He became increasingly aware of the crowd growing quiet, all watching this exchange, and his cock twitched as masculine pride filled him. She whimpered just for him when he took both her wrists, pinning them to the table as he licked up the salt. He then licked over the line from her jean shorts to her navel, gingerly, dragging each moment out until she trembled harder. When he reached her belly button, he slurped up the bitter shot, and dragged his tongue the rest of the way up, licking the salt. He slowed between her breasts before he stopped at her collar bone. Hard, and ready to take this back to his cabin, he gave her a nip, causing her to lift her hips a little, making contact with his body as he bit the lemon. He sucked it. Then he dragged his nose along her neck, until his mouth was just over hers. He hovered there, letting her make the decision. "Your move," he told her, huskily.

And she made it. She reached up and closed her mouth over his.

The crowd erupted into loud applause.

He gave her a good and proper kiss, her tongue swirling against his tequila covered mouth, until she wrapped her legs around him, nearly rocking herself against him. He chuckled against her mouth. *One touch.* And she was now putty in his hands. That was why Miles had come. For this reason alone. This reaction from her had haunted him for months. Nothing came close to the way she brought heat to the blood in his veins.

Miles gathered her in his arms and then lowered her from the bar, purposely dragging her along his rock-hard length, allowing her to feel what she did to him. He hadn't come on this cruise to play fair. He'd come for answers. To find out why she was so damn unforgettable.

Her lips were puffy from his kiss. Her pliable body his for the taking as she thrust her fingers into his hair. "It worked."

"What's that?" he asked, brushing his mouth across hers.

"I want you."

At that, he grinned. "And you can have me."

BY THE TIME Miles got Liv inside his cabin, she could barely contain the wild lust that made her clothes feel too tight. He had been on her mind every single day for the last three months. She thought she'd imaged this overwhelming way he made her feel, but that raw feeling was there, pulsating, making her feel wildly out of control. She liked it. Hell, she wanted *more.* There were a hundred reasons to stop this, but they weakened now. Dead. Pain. For so long she'd felt only that, *always* that, but not now. The moment Miles shut the door behind her, she slammed herself into him and claimed his mouth. He seemed momentarily surprised, hitting the wall and wobbling, but he caught her around the waist, and had her yanked against him a second later, his lips crushing hers.

Everything sizzled. Her lips, her tongue, and most of all, her sex, the very place so desperate for his touch. Frantic to feel the way he owned her body in a way no man had done before, she grabbed his tank top, and he immediately helped her, pulling it over his head in that one-handed move men do. He backed away, and she couldn't stop herself from licking her lips in ravenous hunger. Miles was what men hoped they grew up to become. In the alleyway, he'd never undressed. Now she couldn't take her eyes off him. Strong shoulders, soft hair covering his chest, and biceps that bulged with veins that make her weak in the knees. But it was his gaze that did her in. To some, she had no doubt that his eyes seemed hard. Firm. Unyielding. But beneath, she saw the just-for-her heat that simmered. That night at the wedding she knew being with Miles would be a powerful and intoxicating experience. Now that they had full use of a bedroom, she couldn't wait to see what he did with her body.

Urgent to find out, she reached for the button on his shorts, but he snagged her wrist and spun her around until her back pressed into his chest. His mouth dropped to her neck and he kissed her there, softly, sweetly, teasingly. A deep shiver rolled through her. "Truth time," he said firmly in her ear. "Have you thought about me since our night together?"

She dropped her head back against his shoulder,

grinding her bottom against the impressively big and hard length of him. "Yes," she said, not feeling like that was crossing any lines she couldn't uncross.

"Did you shut me out because you're scared?"

She hesitated. He nipped her shoulder, and the answer all but fell from her lips, "Yes."

His touch turned tender as he pressed a soft kiss to her shoulder and then slid his tongue carnally up her neck, leaving her breathless, until he murmured in her ear, "I've thought of you nearly every night. Every time I stroked my cock, you were on my mind." He nipped her ear lobe, igniting another deep shudder. "Did you touch yourself thinking of me?"

She whimpered, dragging her bottom up and down his length, ready to say any damn thing he wanted to hear, as long as he didn't stop. "Yes."

"Did you make yourself come?"

"Yes."

She felt his smile against her neck. "Good girl," he said, huskily. He rid her of her tank top, then her bra, and while he played with her breasts, she wasn't thinking about all the things she said or if they were the wrong thing to say. She only thought of his passionate touch, stealing all the cold insecurities. When he flicked her nipples, then squeezed them tight, a moan she didn't even recognize escaped her. He obviously approved since a hand skimmed down her belly until he flicked open her jean shorts and slid a hand inside.

"Jesus," she breathed at the first touch. Yes, she missed *this.* The way he made her body melt. The way he made her forget about all the things that could go wrong.

He groaned when he met her silky warmth. "So fucking wet, Liv." His teeth grazed her neck. "Fuck, I've missed this sweet pussy."

Her eyes rolled back into her head.

"Tell me, gorgeous," he said throatily in her ear. "What do you need? My fingers...just like this..." He swirled her little bud, feeding the pleasure, her legs trembling. "Is that what you want from me, Liv?"

"No," she breathed, as he stroked his finger through her soft, wet folds. "More."

"My cock?" he growled in her ear. "That's what you want?"

This time, he pressed her clit, and she could feel her pulse there, the need coursing through her. "Yes. Fuck, yes."

His hands were gone. His breath gone. His nearness gone. All replaced by a firm voice behind her. "Take off your shorts and panties, and I'll give you want you need."

She felt the world spin a little as she tucked her fingers into her shorts and pulled them, along with her panties, down. He had moved to his suitcase, and she watched him open a new box of condoms and take one out before he turned back to her. Her breath hitched at the intensity staring back at her, the way he commanded the space was nothing she'd ever experienced before. Miles knew himself. He trusted his judgment. He saw through bullshit, right to what mattered. And beneath that stare, she felt more vulnerable than ever before. Almost as if he knew how to bare her soul, get it right there in his hands, until she could hide nothing.

His mouth twitched at whatever he saw on her expression. "You're looking a little unsteady there, sweetheart."

"You're…a lot," she admitted.

"A lot of what?" he asked, closing the distance.

"A lot of *man.*"

"Good." He latched onto her hand and yanked her against the hard lines of his body. "Because you're a lot of sweet, warm woman, and you're exactly who I want." She sank into that statement as he sealed his mouth over hers, and she became lost in the talent of his tongue as he stroked hers with more than passion. It was like every move was meant to learn a little more about her. Discover all of her *on* buttons until he knew exactly how to work her body. And damn, did she want to get worked over. Fully, completely, until she screamed his name.

She felt him ditch his shorts and apply the condom before he had her back in his arms and against his chest, her bare ass pressed against his condom-covered cock. The king-sized bed was right there, but he skipped it, nudging her out the open balcony doors with their long white curtains waving in the wind. Immediately, the warm breeze washed over her, followed by the laughter and voices drifting in the air. Her nipples puckered, regardless of the heat outside. People would hear them, and the thrill of that unexpectedly shot straight through her.

Miles cupped her breasts, pinching her taut nipples. "Grab the railing."

"But people could see us?"

He slid his hand between her legs, working her clit. "Does that frighten you? Excite you?"

She moaned, dropping her head back at the pleasure. "Both," she said, shocking herself with her answer.

He didn't respond, simply swirled the bud between her thighs, working her pleasure, until her legs began to tremble. "Grab the railing," he repeated. "Don't let go, no matter how hard you come."

She shivered against him at his promise, doing as instructed, but glancing down, realizing that all anyone had to do was look up and they'd see her. She'd never been this bold, this daring, and yet she was soaking wet with need. More than that, she *wanted* someone to look up and catch a look at them. She realized she wanted to feel something exciting, instead of feeling like a woman she didn't know anymore.

He nudged her legs open and bent her over the railing, and then every inch of him entered her. She gasped at the slight pinch. The sheer size of him filled her impossibly and perfectly all at once. He trailed his fingernails down her back as he withdrew, slowly, carefully, while he gave her time to adjust to him. But that softness didn't last. Soon, he slid in and out effortlessly, and all gentleness vanished. He rocked into her, and his hand soon slid up the back of her neck until he fisted her hair. God, he felt strong. Like nothing could touch her here. He simply wouldn't allow it. And every thrust forward made her feel owned and wanted in the best way possible.

One hand gripped her hip, and he angled her head back, murmuring in her ear, "This was how I imagined taking you when I booked the cruise. Right here, making your scream loud enough for everyone to hear. Is that what you'd like, Liv? To scream? To come?"

"Yes." She gasped.

He thrust hard once, teasing her with what would come. She shivered against him, body quaking against the pleasure he built. "Then come," he growled, but before he moved again, he added, "Let everyone hear how good I fuck you."

She couldn't. She wouldn't. She didn't have a choice as he closed his hard body around hers, enveloping her with his strength. Her hips were pushed up tight against the railing, her breasts hanging over for anyone to see if they looked up, while he pounded her from behind. She fought to stay quiet, but she slowly opened her eyes, catching a couple watching them below. The heat they watched her with, like she was the most beautiful woman in the world, undid her. She thought she should feel embarrassed. That's not what happened.

Her climax hit, surprising her and thrilling her all the same. Her scream no doubt drawing more attention, as her muscles tightened once and then everything exploded until never-ending pleasure stole her away.

MILES LEFT THE bathroom, the steam from his hot shower following him. He stopped short when he caught sight of Liv in bed. She was on her side, her cell phone in her hand, and his gaze traveled along the perfect line from the tip of her toe up her thigh and over the gentle curve of her hipbone. His cock hardened swiftly, and he groaned. "Let's get out of here for a little bit."

She lowered the phone, giving him a view of her breasts, pushed together perfectly. "Everything okay?"

He chuckled, gesturing down at his erection beneath his towel. "We need to talk, and you're making it very hard for me to do that."

"Oh," she said, even though her smile told him she didn't mind the compliment. With her gaze holding his seductively, she slid out of bed, boldly striding toward him, showing him every spectacular curve. "Wouldn't want to interrupt that talk you want to have, would we?"

He gave her a very appreciative once-over, noting her taut nipples even though the room was warm. When he finally looked into her eyes, he spotted the desire there...the *need*. "Are you purposely distracting me Liv, to avoid our talk?"

"No, whatever do you mean?" she said with a sweet smile.

The Dom in him would have tied her the bed and teased her mercilessly until she realized what happened when she taunted him. But the man in him loved that smile, that playful nature. He grinned back. "You're a clever, clever woman."

Her laughter echoed around him as he scooped her up and dropped her back onto the bed. And instead of teasing her, he gave himself what he wanted. *Her.*

By the time they left the cabin, Miles was sure he couldn't make her any more satisfied than she already was. He was dead wrong.

"Oh, my sweet God," Liv purred. She licked her lips at the rows of ice cream, in front of another row of sundae toppings. "I had no idea this even existed."

Miles smiled, nudging her forward with a hand on

the small of her back. He'd overheard two women talking about the midnight ice cream bar when he'd first arrived on the ship, and he figured Liv would appreciate it too. He was glad he got that right. When he reached the bowls, he offered her one and moved out of her way.

She started with vanilla ice cream, then added a scoop of chocolate, which soon disappeared beneath the hot fudge, sprinkles, peanut butter cups, peanuts, and every other thing she could find. Following her lead, Miles didn't skimp either.

When Liv was finished, she grabbed napkins and spoons, and Miles followed her outside. A seating area with small iron tables and chairs had been set under rows of twinkling string lights. Plants situated around the space made it feel like they were in some backyard garden in Tuscany, not sitting on a cruise ship. Farther down, another couple ate quietly, moaning in happiness.

Miles held out the chair for Liv, and she quickly dug right in. "Oh my God, this is…"

"Good," Miles finished for her, after he took his first bite. He wiped the napkin across his mouth, seeing a chocolate smear on her bottom lip. He nearly leaned across the table and licked it off, but figured they needed to talk. He scooped up more ice cream with his spoon. "Are your friends all right with you being with me tonight?" The last thing he wanted to do was cause a rift.

She shoved her spoon with the gooey hot fudge into

her mouth and simply nodded. Once she finished her bite, she replied, "We've got a chat group. That's who I was talking with when you came out of the shower. They're all doing their own thing tonight with people they've met, and we're meeting up for breakfast in the morning. We're good."

"I'm glad," he said, lowering his spoon back to his bowl. "So, now that you've ruled out your college friends from sending the email, any other idea who could be behind it?"

She finished her spoonful and then shrugged. "I have no idea."

Miles didn't have any reason not to trust her judgment. "What about Allie?"

"I mean, maybe," Liv finally answered with another shrug. She slid her spoon back through the ice cream, scooping up some peanuts on her way. "But I just can't see Allie ever doing something so…"

"Bold?" Miles offered.

"Yeah, bold and intrusive." Liv nodded. "She just doesn't get involved in my life like that, no matter how many times I talked to her about you." Her lips immediately clamped shut, obviously regretting her words.

Miles couldn't help the twitch of his mouth. Yeah, he'd talked about her too. "Well," he said, having what he needed to move the conversation along. "It's pretty damn clear that whoever sent me the email is playing matchmaker."

"Seems so," she admitted.

He placed his spoon back in the bowl, rested both arms on the table, and leveled her with a hard look. "Which brings me to my next point: why would someone go to all this trouble to get us onto this cruise ship together?"

The answer was right there on her face, and she surprised him this time by actually saying it. "Probably because they think it'll make me happy."

He hesitated, watching her, not quite sure if he should push or not. His gut told him to push, albeit gently. "Which begs the question, have you not been happy lately?"

She looked at her ice cream bowl. "I'm fine."

Miles knew with total certainty that meant not fine at all.

He waited her out, and she eventually lifted her soft eyes to him. "It's just...that night, with us...well, it was hard to forget. That's all."

Miles grinned. "I'm that unforgettable, huh?"

"Don't go getting a big head about it," she said with a laugh, the hair around her face fluttering in the light breeze.

He laughed with her, certain he'd never seen anyone so beautiful. "Then help me understand all this," he said, letting his smile fall. "I made it very clear I wanted to see you again. Why didn't you let me come out and visit?"

She shifted uneasily in her seat. "Because there are obstacles in our way. Big ones. You live in Vegas. I'm in San Fran. It seemed silly to start something when it couldn't ever work."

"Those are only obstacles if it's impossible to move."

"It *is* impossible to move," she said. "For one, my life is in San Francisco. My friends. My job. For another, I'm really close to my family. My mom has multiple sclerosis, and this last year has been rough for her. She's in a wheelchair now."

He saw the pain in her face. Even heard it in her voice. "I'm sorry to hear that."

"Thanks," she said with a little shrug. "It's hard, but my mom's strong as hell. She's got a really positive attitude about it all."

Now he understood. "I see why moving would be hard for you, but why are you so dead set that someone couldn't move for you?"

She held his gaze. Firmly. "Because I would never let someone do that for me."

"What if that choice wasn't yours to make?"

She glanced to her bowl with a sigh before looking at him again. "I would never let it get that far where someone had to make that choice. Love has got to make sense, or someone is going to be hurt."

"And that won't be you?"

She lifted her chin. "That's right."

"I take it that resolve comes from the broken heart you told me about at the wedding?"

She shrugged and focused back on her ice cream, scooping up more on her spoon.

In his life, he wasn't used to having to push or navigate to get the answers he needed. And somehow, he liked how she kept parts of herself shielded away. She wasn't easy to understand. She made him work to get to know her. She was a challenge he didn't even know he wanted.

"No more bullshit. No more games," he told her, and she set her spoon down, giving him her full attention, as he added, "Here's where I'm at with this. It's been three months since I met you, and I want you as much now as I did that night at the wedding. Absolutely nothing has changed for me. There's something between us that's real and rare, and I want to explore it and see where we end up. With that being said, I'd like to propose something to you."

She studied him. Hard. "What's that?"

"Give me these six days," he said boldly. "Shut off that gorgeous mind of yours. Don't think about all the complications, or the impossibility of things, about if and how this will work in the future, just be here in the present and enjoy these days with me."

"And then what?" she asked.

He laughed dryly and shook his head. "You can't even shut off your mind for a minute." He intertwined his strong fingers with her delicate ones, and then turned her hand over, palm up. He slowly dragged his thumb across her wrist, captivated by the way her pupils dilated under his touch. "Neither of us can have that answer because there's no possible way to see where we'll be at the end of the cruise. All I know is, there's something here." She shivered, and he gave her a knowing smile. "There was something here from the second our eyes met at the wedding. And there was something again when I saw you yesterday. After tonight, I know I need more. I want more of you. What do we have to lose?" He rose, leaned across the table and slid a finger across her jawline, loving how heat rushed into her gaze. "I've had you three times and look how fucking good it's been. Imagine how it'll be when I truly know your body."

A beat passed between them. "You're a Dominant."

He placed both hands on the table, staring into the strength of her eyes, the determination there to shut him out. He wondered if she'd heard that about him and Club Sin from Allie, but he realized he didn't mind that she knew. It saved a long and awkward conversation. He inclined his head. "I am a Dominant."

"I'm not a submissive," she said. "Nor do I have an exciting sex life like I'm sure you're used to."

He leaned in, inhaling her rich scent that drove him wild with need, and leveled her with a hard look. "There is more than one type of submissive, Liv."

She cocked her head. "What do you mean?"

"I fucked you in an alleyway at a wedding, and I just

fucked you on a balcony. The second you saw others were watching, you came." Her face burned bright red, which he smiled at. Hell, she was cute. "You're adventurous, but obviously haven't been given the chance to explore. You submit your body to me naturally when I touch you. You followed every direction I gave you on the balcony, and willingly wanted to. Why do you think that wouldn't be enough for me?"

"Because I don't know you."

He gave a firm nod. "My point exactly. Let's take these six days to get to know each other. At the end of those six days, we'll face the complications head on or we won't because we'll know this was something fun between us and that's it. We'll go home back to our lives and can firmly say that it just isn't going to work." He cupped her cheek, sliding a thumb across her pouty lips. "But to do that, you have to stop shutting me out. Can you do that?"

She leaned into him and rasped, "Six days together?"

"Six of the hottest days of our lives," he murmured, knowing the risks. One night with Liv had ruined him for three months. What would six days do? But when she melted beneath his hands, he knew she was worth the risk. "Just give me the word I need to hear."

She rose to meet him across the table, and just before her lips met his, she whispered, "Yes."

CHAPTER 5

THE NEXT MORNING, Liv left Miles behind to meet Grace, Benjamin, Aubrey, and Kendall at the buffet breakfast. Last night sat heavy on her mind. If being with Miles showed her one thing it was that her world was small, and if she looked at her life from the outside, there were flaws. She once had dreams of becoming a real estate agent herself. She once loved love. Where did all that go? Why wasn't she living more adventurously? She needed answers to these questions, and her gut told her she'd find those answers with Miles. He had been unforgettable, but it was the way he made her feel that stood out. She wanted to be this sensual, exciting woman she was when she was with him. The woman she *could* be, even if it was only for six days.

At noon, the ship would dock in Orlando and Miles wanted to take her on a day date in the city. But first, she needed to get to breakfast. She was beginning to feel like the world's worst friend. When she finally entered the restaurant, she found her friends sitting at a table, already eating. She gave them all a quick wave before she hastily moved to the buffet and filled her plate with bacon, eggs, and a couple waffles with syrup before approaching the table. "Where's Aubrey?" she asked, taking a seat next to Benjamin.

"MIA," he said.

"Anyone text her to make sure she's okay?" Not that Aubrey wasn't well known for being MIA. It might have well been her middle name.

Grace finished her sip of her coffee and said, "I did. She said she's busy, but she'll be here soon."

"Busy or getting busy?" Liv asked, reaching for her napkin and placing it on her lap.

"The latter, I'm sure," Kendall said. "But the *who* is up for debate."

Liv added a couple sugars to her coffee. Aubrey had a coffee, too, but Liv suspected it'd be cold by the time she got here.

"How's everything going with Miles?" Kendall asked. "Is he the stalker I thought he was?"

Liv laughed softly. "No, not a stalker. Everything is hot and actually kind of good. I'm probably in way over my head here, but all he wants is to spend time with me while we're on the cruise. And well…the sex is…"

"Mind-blowing?" Kendall asked with a full mouth.

Liv nodded. "Intense."

"Well, I say, good for you," Benjamin said. "You've been shutting this guy out for months. There is nothing wrong with having a wild affair and that being the end of it."

"Cheers to that," Liv said, then clanged glasses with Benjamin.

Of course, the sensible Grace pipped up. "But will that be the end of it?"

"It's got to be," Liv said. "You all know how I feel about this."

"You don't date men who are bad for you," they all said in unison.

Liv nodded happily, even though apparently, she'd been drilling that line into them, and she wasn't exactly sure what that said about her. "Exactly. I mean, really, who spends six days together and then decides to move to be with that person? It's just not going to happen. I weighed the risk, and it's impossible that anyone is going to get hurt here. He's not asking to date me. He's asking for six hot days together. I'd be an idiot to say no to that."

"You're right, you would," Benjamin agreed.

Liv smiled at him and then decided she'd told enough of her secrets for one breakfast. "All right, since everyone knows about me and Miles," she said to the group, "do you guys plan on telling me who you all are hooking up with?"

Blank stares met hers, and Liv laughed. "Yeah, no one is getting off the hook here. I've told you *everything*.

Tell me about the guy you met," she said to Kendall.

"What?" Kendall blinked.

Liv pointed her fork at her. "Who is he?"

Kendall's cheeks stained with dark red hues.

"Oh, he's Alex Jeffries, and Grace has a hottie warming up her bed too," Benjamin said.

Grace choked on the water she was drinking. She coughed as she set it back down on the table. "His name is Bryan Sirimongkol, not 'hottie'." She lifted her chin, looking ever so stoic and put together as always. "Why don't you tell Liv everything about Lucas Hall, Benjamin?"

Benjamin grinned a smile of pure sex. "He's an assistant football coach, tall, green eyed. Gorgeous."

"Sounds yummy," Liv said, nibbling her bacon.

"Scrumptious," Benjamin agreed.

Liv smiled and then sighed. "So, there's something I want to talk about with you all. Miles wants to take me into Orlando on a day date, but if anyone—"

Again, nearly in unison, everyone said, "We're busy too."

Liv laughed and slowly shook her head. "You all realize that we're failing epically at having a friend reunion?"

"Sex, Liv," Benjamin stated. Then he gave her one of his sweet smiles. "We'll all always be friends, and we'll be better about getting together, but right now this cruise is shaping up to be something none of us expected. Let's go with it."

Liv glanced around and everyone else nodded. She supposed they hadn't changed that much over the years. No one passed up a good time. "Okay, then, that's settled. Let's try and meet up every day, though? Breakfast. Dinner. Deal?"

"Deal," the group responded.

With that all settled, she dug into her food, as did the others, and the conversation shifted to avoid talking about their current hook ups. No one in their group of friends was very good at relationships, long-term or short. But Liv wondered if someone would find love here. She reached for her coffee and took a long sip, hoping one of her friends did. No matter how much time passed since she saw her college friends, their bond never wavered. They all deserved good things. The best things.

Just as she swallowed her coffee, her stomach screaming at her to stop eating, Grace's gasp made her look up.

Aubrey strode up to the table with Carter Hayes, the famous Hollywood actor, at her side. He was trying very hard not to look like Carter Hayes. His Iowa farm boy disguise wasn't fooling anyone. He had blond hair, blue eyes created to-die-for, looks that couldn't be ignored. Liv outright gawked, unable to help it. Aubrey had a Carter Hayes thirst account on Instagram. Her crushing levels on Carter topped red-hot, and fate was working some serious magic on this cruise. Liv blinked a few times just to make sure her eyes weren't betraying her.

They weren't. Both of them still had damp hair, and he had a tiny bite mark at the base of his throat.

She glanced around the table, finding bemused shock on her friends' faces. Aubrey began nibbling her lip nervously. Liv quickly intervened and broke the silence to save Aubrey. "Imagine you two rolling in late together."

"Our rooms are right next to each other," Aubrey said.

A total lie. Even Benjamin covered his chuckle with a coughing fit.

Liv rose and turned, putting her back to Carter and mouthed to Aubrey, *"What are you doing?"*

"Him," Aubrey mouthed back. Liv blinked, realizing that her and Miles's situation wasn't nearly as complicated as Aubrey's. She felt oddly refreshed by that as Aubrey stepped closer and whispered, "I'm in way over my head."

Liv snorted. "Believe me, you're not the only one."

And almost on cue, from behind her, Miles said by way of greeting, "Good morning."

Liv turned around, hit by the heat he brought, even if he was currently looking at her group of friends. "Hi," she said. His gaze met hers then, and the smile he gave her took her breath away.

"Hi." He leaned in a pressed a sweet kiss on her cheek that didn't feel so sweet. "Have the plans for the day been decided?"

She nodded. "We can go into Orlando, if you'd like."

"Excellent." He grinned. Then he addressed her friends. "You all don't mind if I steal Liv away for the day?"

Benjamin gave a sly grin. "Bring her back as glowing as she was this morning, then we'll be just fine."

Miles glanced sideways at Liv. "Now that I can do."

Liv's nipples puckered at the promise, making her not regret her decision to enjoy these days with him. He offered his hand and she twined her fingers with his as she asked, "Are you going to tell me what we're doing today?"

He grinned devilishly. "Nope."

"A secret, huh?" She smiled in return.

"One I bet you'll never figure out."

She tried. Hard. The whole drive in the Uber from the dock to downtown Orlando in the Central Business District, and every answer she guessed was wrong. She gave up asking when they reached Orlando's Financial District, which held all the major banks, night clubs, restaurants, and modern commercial towers. But the charm of this city was the mix of the new and old, with historical buildings set next to modern skyscrapers.

Just as she exited the car, her cell phone rang. A quick look at the screen revealed it was Allie. "Do you mind if I take this?" she asked Miles.

"Of course not." He left her near the street while he approached the door of an old, Queen Anne-style building.

Liv turned away and answered the Facetime call. "Oh my God, I've been dying to talk to you."

Allie sat at her desk at work, a wall of windows behind her. Her long brown hair pulled up into a messy top bun, and the unruly strands spoke of a long day. Considering it was early into the afternoon, that wasn't a good sign.

"I'm sorry," Allie said. "I meant to call earlier. It's been a day. Lots of meetings."

Liv knew that tone. The tightness around Allie's sharp blue eyes. "What happened?"

"The Roy deal went south." The deal had been for a multi-million dollar home.

"Shit, really? Dammit. I should be there to help you," Liv said. The dark circles under Allie's eyes said she needed her.

"Oh, please, stop it. You deserve a vacation. This was an unexpected hiccup that you don't need to worry about. But how about you tell me why you called me this morning on your vacation?"

"Miles is here."

Allie blinked. Twice. "Miles is where?"

"Here. On the cruise ship." She quickly caught Allie up, finishing up with, "And now we're in Orlando about to go on a day date. So, tell me, and please be honest, I won't be mad, was it you who sent the email inviting him?"

Allie's eyes were huge. "Of course not, I'd never do that to you. Everything you told me about him is locked up tight. I'd never break that trust, you know that. I never even told Micah."

Liv didn't push. She never thought it'd be Allie anyway. That simply wasn't her best friend's way. Their friendship was a vault that came with an unbreakable lock. "All right then, if it's not you, who in the hell is behind this?"

Allie shrugged, but then her expression shifted, a knowing look crossing her face.

"What do you know?" Liv pressed.

Allie nibbled her lip. "I might be pulling this out of nowhere, but I know that Miles's friend, Porter, owns a private investigation firm. Maybe he did some digging and found out you were going on this cruise and they arranged all this."

Liv considered that. "A possibility for sure, but that theory would only work if they had known I couldn't stop thinking about him. And I don't know any of them."

"True," Allie agreed, nibbling her lip again. "Sorry, babe, I've got nothing for you. What a weird situation."

"Tell me about it." Liv glanced over her shoulder, finding Miles leaning against the railing, scrolling through his cell phone. "Okay, the short story, I've agreed to spend these six days with him. Please tell me if I'm making a huge mistake? Is this going to end in my heart breaking into a million pieces?"

Allie shook her head, softly. "You've got to let those fears go. Not *everything* is going to end in disaster."

But it did.

Allie added, "In fact, I'd say this is maybe the smartest thing you've ever done for yourself. Six hot days and nights with the most incredible sex of your life sounds pretty damn good. And you can finally see if there is really something going on between you two, or you walk away and forget him for good." She hesitated, cocking her head. "Maybe this is exactly what you need. Three months is a long time to think about someone who you were only with once. Fate's at work here, babe. Follow it."

The tension sitting on Liv's chest instantly lifted. That's what talking to Allie did. "Okay, yes, you're right. This is good. Fun. I deserve this."

"Atta girl." Allie smiled. "Have way too much naughty fun."

"You know it." Liv laughed softly. "Bye."

"Bye." Allie ended the call.

Warmth and comfort touched Liv's chest. Allie just got her, and always made Liv so much more at ease. The truth was, Liv knew she was often led by fear, as sad as that was. She couldn't help but wonder what would happen if she let go and just…*lived.* A long sigh spilled from her mouth as she turned around to Miles, finding his attention still on his phone. "It wasn't Allie who sent you the email," she called as she approached.

Miles lifted his head, perplexed. "The mystery remains unsolved then." He slid his cell back into his pocket.

Liv nodded, and sidled up next to him on the steps of the historic building. "Could it be one of your friends? Allie said you know a private investigator."

Miles didn't even hesitate, his mouth twitching. "Not a chance in hell."

"You're *that* sure?"

"Yes, I'm that sure. My close friends are Dominants. We are ruled by a code of honor. They would never cross that line and interfere with my life."

"Never?"

"Never."

"Okay," she said, beginning to wonder if it even mattered anymore why Miles ended up on the cruise. She studied the building behind her. From the outside, it looked like a nightclub, maybe. The windows were dark, blinds covering them. "So, is now the time you tell me where you've brought me?"

"Sure," he said, gesturing at the building. "We're at Orlando's elite sex club."

"You're kidding?" she asked with a nervous laughter.

"Not kidding," he said, calmly. "Would you like to go inside and explore?"

She studied the building, reassessing, feeling her heartrate spike and her skin flush at the idea of the eroticism that was waiting for her on the other side of that doorway. And yet, she felt frozen at the idea of doing anything so daring. Scared that if she walked through that door, Miles would see how boring she truly was compared to the women in the club. "What if we don't go in?" she asked, turning back to Miles.

"Then we skip the club and I take you out for a romantic lunch date I've got planned too," he said. "That's what these six days are all about, figuring out if this thing between us extends past this amazing connection we've got going on." He stuck a thumb under her chin, locking her into his potent stare. "If you don't want to go in, then we don't. If we go in and you hate what you see, we leave. No questions asked. But I think you'll enjoy watching others. You certainly enjoyed being watched."

She did like it. Far more than she would have ever

believed. There was something about being put on display, knowing others got off because they thought she was beautiful and sexy. That excited her. "Is that what you want to happen, us to have sex in front of others?" Dear God, she had to force those words out.

He shook his head. "You make the rules here, Liv, not me."

She glanced at the building's wooden door again, feeling like if she walked through, she'd leave the old her behind and find someone new. Oddly enough, she realized she wasn't afraid. She wanted to know.

At whatever crossed her expression, Miles cocked his head, brushing his thumb across her lips. "I need the words, Liv. Tell me what you want."

This time, she didn't hesitate. "I want to go inside."

CHAPTER 6

M ILES ENTERED THE classy sex club, The Lounge, and lust was practically vibrating in the large, open space. Sex and freedom and powerful connections brushed across his senses, kicking up his heartrate. The owner, Phillip Boucher, had lived in Las Vegas for many years and had been a member of Club Sin. When Phillip moved out to Orlando and opened his own club, Miles had visited. He enjoyed his visit immensely, but nothing could touch the emotions building in him when he walked through the doors holding Liv's hand and seeing the innocence all but bursting out of her when she took in the sexually-charged room.

The lounge itself was well put together. The exposed stone walls and open space gave a full view of the sexual exchanges going on in the room. There were three shows happening. On the one large, round bed, an orgy of ten people were indulging in sensual playtime. Across from them, a man was bound to a chair with rope and was currently experiencing a blowjob from two lingerie clad curvy women. And in the far corner, a woman was bound to a saint Andrew's cross. Miles watched that scene with interest, not approving of the way the submissive flinched against the flicks of the flogger the Dominant sent her way. By the quickness of her breathing, the redness of her skin, she'd been there for some time. It looked to him that she was not enjoying herself, nor was she accepting the pleasure being offered to her. He frowned and then looked at Liv, finding her eye was caught by something else. She stared toward the bar off to the right, where leather wingback chairs rested. In one of them was a man who always stood out in a crowd.

Phillip Boucher. His styled blond hair, playful blue-eyes, and lean muscular body caught the eyes of many ladies, but it was the French accent that worked better than an aphrodisiac.

Phillip's attention was glued to the scene that caught Miles's attention too. His eyes narrowed on the woman's reaction. At their approach, Phillip looked over.

"Miles, you've finally arrived. Please come," said Phillip in his thick accent, calling Miles forward with a wave of his hand.

Miles kept Liv's sweaty palm in his and led her toward Phillip, who sat between two beautiful blondes, with a brunette kneeling at his feet.

Liv's gaze went to the woman kneeling, and Miles saw her face go blank. He assumed she felt rude, so she shut down.

Miles turned back to Phillip as he asked, "Qui est ce plaisir?" *Who is this treat?*

"Un ami," Miles replied. *A friend.*

Phillip's heady gaze raked over Liv, while his hand stroked the woman on his left thigh. "Innocent?"

"Assez." *Quite.*

Liv moved a little closer to Miles, and Phillip's mouth twitched. "Peut-être pas seulement un ami." *Perhaps not just a friend.*

Miles returned the grin. "Peut-être." *Perhaps.*

Phillip's voice softened when he spoke in English again. He smiled gently at Liv. "Please enjoy yourself in my club, sweet one. Your fantasies await you here."

"Thank you," she said after a deep swallow.

Miles held back his smile. She *was* sweet. That was true. He squeezed her hand, proud of her for not shrinking in an awkward moment. The first time in a sex club was rattling even for the most adventurous. "Thanks for the invite, Phillip. Always good to see you."

Phillip flashed his charming grin. "You're always welcome, Miles."

Before Miles headed off, he took another look at that woman on the Saint Andrew's Cross, saw another flinch, then addressed Phillip. "My apologies for taking your attention away from your club."

"Yes, I must go deal with that." Phillip was on his

feet a second later and let out a string of French curse words before heading off to the security guard who was chatting to a gorgeous redhead instead of keeping an eye on the scene. Phillip was there in a second, stopped the scene, and ripped the security guard a new one before he snapped his fingers, another Dominant there, taking the other's place. The new Dominant strode up, stroked the woman's stomach, softly, and Miles saw her long, slow breath.

"What was that all about?" Liv asked, obviously confused by the exchange.

Miles glanced her way, stroking his thumb over her hand. "That woman wasn't enjoying herself. She's either too strong to say her safe word, which would have ended the scene, or she doesn't truly know what she wants and needs. You see that security guard Phillip is currently tearing into?"

Liv's gaze followed his. "Yeah."

"He should have seen what was happening there and stopped the scene."

Liv's head cocked. Her inquisitive eyes came to him. "How did you know something was wrong?"

"I pay attention." He enjoyed how she leaned into him a little, showing a bit of trust when he led her away in the opposite direction. "You must have more questions."

She didn't even hesitate. "Yeah, I do. You speak

French?"

Of all the questions to ask first, he liked that she wanted to know more about him. He stopped before they moved into the crowd. "My mother was born in France. She lived there until she was twenty before moving to the United States. She was vigilant I learn French growing up."

"It's a beautiful language," Liv said, and then leveled him with a gorgeous smile. "Does your French mother know you come to places like this?"

He laughed. "That's very unlikely. Besides, I don't see my parents very often. They have dual citizenship and moved back to France after I left the house."

At that, her eyes turned sad. "You've got no other family in Vegas then?"

"I've got found family," he replied. "My friends are closer to me than brothers." Knowing part of her conversation was deflection, he turned them back onto the club again. "What are your first thoughts about this place? Is it what you expected it to be?"

She glanced out and gave a rough laugh. "It's a lot to take in."

"It is," he agreed with a nod.

"I mean, some of this, I'm just like...whoa, that's really hot," she admitted, glancing at the man bound to the chair. "But some of it, I can never see myself doing."

"Like what?"

She glanced back at the woman kneeling on the floor, silent, waiting for Phillip to return. "I couldn't do that. Be subordinate like that. It's just…" Her worried eyes came to him. "I don't have that me."

"And you don't have to have that in you," he reassured her. "Erotic play is about limits, trust, and most importantly, it should be fun and enjoyable. You've got to like what you're doing or what is the point of doing it?" He gestured to the kneeling woman again. "I suspect she feels peace there. Maybe being quiet is very hard for her. Maybe she needs to be on the move all the time. And Phillip, as her Dominant, is giving her what she needs."

Liv studied the woman, curiosity brimming in her eyes. "Okay, I guess that makes sense." She threw him another firm look. "Still not in me, though."

He chuckled. "Let's see what is then, shall we?" He nudged her forward into the crowd, and the second Miles caught sight of the blonde coming out on stage, he knew he had to thank Phillip later. His friend was more than generous. The innocence in the blonde's wide eyes, the quick breaths she took, her bright red cheeks, told Miles this was her first time in the club.

"Come with me," Miles said, taking Liv's hand. "Let's watch this one."

She squeezed his hand tight and followed behind.

When they reached the edge of the crowd, he moved

in behind her, sliding an arm around her middle, keeping her close, as a dark-haired man joined the woman on stage. This Dominant wasn't unskilled like the other. He had this woman all but begging for his touch, and he'd barely even gotten started. "This is the connection between a Dominant and a woman sexually submitting to him," Miles told Liv in her ear. "Do you see it? How she's moving? How she's breathing? Can you see how she's begging for more with her body, without saying a single word?"

"Yes, I see that," Liv said softly, amazement in her voice.

"People always think kink is rough and, and of course, for some, it is that."

"But not for you?"

"No, Liv, not me." He slid his hand across her belly overtop of her dress. "For me, it's about this." She shivered, and he smiled, brushing his mouth across her ear. "The connection. The exploration of two souls meeting and sharing something only they can experience together." He kissed her neck and chuckled as she wiggled her ass into him, her body ripening, readying for him. "It's about tearing the fabric of each other's fucking worlds apart and reforming it into something new. Something stronger."

The dance between the Dominant and submissive on stage continued with hot touches until the flogger came out. This woman wasn't flinching, she was moving toward the leather tails, accepting, being brought higher. Until even Miles saw her hard trembles. Then the Dominant opened his pants, sheathed himself in a condom and bent the woman over a spanking bench, taking her roughly.

Miles felt Liv's body tighten with anticipation. "What does seeing this do to you?" he asked in her ear.

"Turns me on," she breathed, leaning her head back against him, softening, welcoming…"Makes me want you."

He grasped her hip with one hand, then trailed his fingers along her thigh, slowly dragging her dress up as he went. Her breathing grew ragged as that touch worked its way across her sex. He tickled there, played, teasing her, and she began trembling. Only when she moaned his name did he draw her dress up and slip his fingers inside her panties.

She slid her hand up to cup his neck as he stroked gently over her clit.

"Widen your legs for me," he murmured.

She obeyed and he slid lower, meeting the warm silky wetness. "I want to have you, Liv," he murmured in her ear. "Right here, in front of all these people, show them how goddamn lucky I am that I get to touch you. Show them how beautiful you are when you fall apart in my arms."

She wiggled her ass into him. An invitation?

"I need the words, Liv," he said.

She leaned her head back and moaned, "Have me."

"Lift your dress and move your panties aside," he ordered.

She did as he asked, while he wasted no time grabbing a condom from his wallet. In quick time he had his cock free from his zipper and sheathed. With a hand on her hip, he entered her from behind. Miles's arm brushed against the man next to him. People on either side all focused on the show in front of them. "Do you want them to turn and watch you?" he murmured in her ear. "For you to be the center of attention now?"

"Yes," she rasped, her legs trembling against his.

"All you need to do is moan, Liv." He nipped her ear. "Moan and let them hear you, and they'll see how beautiful you are." He moved slowly, letting her feel all of him, while he felt all of her. He slid his hand up and cupped her breast, when suddenly she moaned. Loud.

He could feel some eyes in the crowd shift to them. Feel Liv's inner walls clench tight when she realized it too.

And at that, it came as absolutely no surprise when she rose in her pleasure. She liked having eyes on her, as much as he did, even if she wasn't ready to admit that aloud. Miles knew she was locked up tight, bound by her pain, but with every touch, every moment she allowed herself under his command, he felt those binds loosen.

He dropped his mouth to her neck, bit at the fleshly part of her shoulder and felt her shudder against him, her body hugging him tight. He squeezed her breast before moving on to the other, his fingers tightening on her hip, holding her firmly to him as her knees weakened. He caught movement to his right, and wanting to increase the intensity for her, he said, "Look to your right."

She turned, the pleasure washing over her face before he felt her body contract around him at the sight before her. He groaned against her tightness, against her perfection, against her ass bouncing with every one of his thrusts. Her focus remained on the couple next to them. The woman kneeling in front of her man, giving him a blowjob, while he watched them. Miles didn't take his eyes off Liv. Off her beauty. Off the magic he felt when her eyes suddenly shut tight. And soon, those slight trembles became hard quakes, and with a loud moan drawing more attention, she broke apart and tumbled into where he took her. But what did surprise him was that he followed her, losing control at the feel of her...the scent of her...the sound of her. Oh, what this woman did to him.

"And *that,* Liv," he murmured in her ear after he emptied himself inside her, "is an introduction into my world."

CHAPTER 7

THE FOLLOWING MORNING, Liv woke up, still riding the high from the club. She could sum up her sex life as 1950's America. Missionary. Boring. Last night her world had been blown apart, and the most mindboggling part of it all, she wanted *more*. She'd never considered herself wild in nature. She'd been too busy with life to really throw herself out there, and she'd come from parents who were so buttoned-up, sometimes even Liv could barely breathe. But last night made everything look unfamiliar, like the world was a place she'd barely even explored. Everything looked new…different. And being with Miles made her wonder; how much of the world had she not seen? She kept waiting to feel dirty by what she'd done, and seen, and she simply didn't. She felt life pulsating through her veins.

After texting Aubrey in desperate need of girl talk, and leaving Miles eating breakfast on his balcony, Liv made it to the breakfast buffet. She found Aubrey already sitting, the sun casting its beams on their table. Liv smiled. Aubrey hadn't changed at all. She'd always been like a cat, finding the sunny spots and staying there as long as she could. Aubrey stared out at the open water, her brows drawn, her teeth worrying her bottom lip. Maybe Liv wasn't the only one who needed this talk. And maybe she wasn't the only one treading a very dangerous line between fantasy and reality.

She and Audrey's friendship had changed over the years and she barely saw Aubrey anymore, but it was still one of the strongest, most familiar relationships in her life. It didn't matter that, when they finished college, Liv moved back home to San Francisco and Aubrey moved back home to Salvation, Virginia. Their bond never wavered.

"Morning," Liv said, reaching the table.

Aubrey finished her sip of mimosa. "Morning. Got you a glass too."

"Yum. Thanks." Liv gestured to the buffet. "I'm starving. You?"

"Hell, yes," said Aubrey, hopping up and following Liv to the buffet.

A few minutes later, Liv had sausages, scrambled eggs, and toast, and every other breakfast food she could fit on her plate. Her body needed the fuel. She hadn't felt as sore as she did now since she'd gone back to the gym a couple years ago. Though she'd take Miles's kind of workout any day.

She returned to the table, and after placing her plate

down, dropped into the seat.

Aubrey said, "So, I take it, by your sparkly self that things with Miles are going well?"

Liv chuckled. "I'm sparkling, huh?"

Aubrey smiled at Liv over the rim of her coffee cup. "As sparkly as those vampires in *Twilight*."

Liv laughed. "Well, there's a very good reason for that," she explained. "Miles took me to a sex club yesterday."

Aubrey spit the coffee back into her mug, coughing. When she could breathe again, she exclaimed, "You went to a sex club?"

Heat rushed over Liv's cheeks, as every head turned in their direction. "Must you yell that?" she blasted back at Aubrey.

"Yes, I must yell that," Aubrey gasped. "This is shocking! I mean, doing something that wild is totally my jam, but you?" She blinked twice. "Who are you and what have you done with my good girl, Liv?"

Liv gave the people watching them a smile she hoped spoke of her apology. "Good girl Liv is on vacation."

Again, Aubrey blinked, sitting unnaturally still. "How on earth did you even find a sex club?" she asked.

"I didn't find one. Miles did. He knows the guy who owns it."

Aubrey placed her hands flat on the table and leaned in, her eyes glued on Liv. "Girl, tell me every single thing that has happened since you set foot on this ship."

Liv took a long sip of her coffee, and then explained it all, from the surprise of seeing Miles there, to the body shot, to the hot sex, to deciding to embrace their days together, to finally learning more about his erotic tastes. "And that brings us to this morning," she finished.

"Wow," Aubrey breathed, chewing on a piece of bacon. "That's just...*wow.* What was it like there?"

"Wild...and kind of amazing too. You know me, I've never been bold like that." She leaned in and whispered, "But I'm telling you, Aubrey, I liked it...you know, having sex there."

Aubrey laughed. "That is so hot."

Liv laughed with her. "It is, but it's also so much. *He's* so much."

Aubrey cocked her head, the sunlight warming the caramel highlights through her hair. "In a bad way?"

"Not bad necessarily," Liv explained after a moment of consideration. "Just intense, you know. It's like all this is fun and sexy, but it's even more than that." She hesitated, then told herself not to. Her heart needed someone to listen. "I feel like I'm falling..."

Aubrey's eyebrows shot up. "Falling in love with him?"

"God, no, I barely even know him," Liv corrected then paused. "I would never fall for him. He still lives in Vegas. I still live in San Francisco. Nothing about the obstacles in our way has changed, but it's more like I'm changing. I don't even know how to explain it. It just feels like I'm different with him. Like, I'm falling into where he wants me to go...making me want things...making me oddly trust him ...making me feel things that I can't control."

Aubrey nibbled her bacon, her eyes turning inquisitive.

"What's with the look?" Liv asked with a laugh.

"Maybe being out of your comfort zone isn't such a bad thing," Aubrey said. "Maybe it's about damn time you did something wild. Maybe Miles is actually the first guy to make you feel something that you can't control. And maybe, this is how real love starts and you shouldn't be so closed off to seeing where this goes with him."

Liv swallowed deeply. "I can't do that again." Being in control kept her heart safe.

"I know," Aubrey said, eyes sad. "But at some point, you're going to have to dive in and believe that everything is going to work out. It's been years since Gavin. This could be your chance to be happy, Liv. Don't turn a blind eye to that."

I have to...she almost replied, but then kept the thought to herself. She'd let go once and it had cost her deeply, when she knew better to let her guard down. She remembered vividly what it felt like to see the world lose its color. To feel so drowned by betrayal and heartbreak that she lost the energy to get out of bed. Aubrey had come to San Francisco during that week after Gavin's cheating came to light. She'd been there through the tears, the anger, and she, along with Allie, gave Liv the love she needed to pick herself up again. The very thought of going through that again made her stomach go laden with her breakfast. "But what if I'm not enough for him?"

Aubrey frowned. "How could you not be enough for him? You're Liv!"

She rolled her eyes. "Oh, I don't know. Maybe because he goes to sex clubs and has women falling at his feet, and I'm...well, not going to fall at his feet."

Aubrey laughed softly. "Maybe he's bored with that kind of thing. You could be refreshing to him."

"Maybe," Liv said after consideration. But that stupid little voice in her head got loud: *You thought you could change Gavin...and he cheated.*

Not hungry anymore, she pushed her plate away, and did what she did best, avoided the subject all together. "Okay, enough about me. What's wrong?"

Aubrey adverted her gaze. "Nothing."

"Liar." Liv pointed her fork at Aubrey. "I know you. You had that *I-am-thinking-deep* look when I showed up. Talk to me."

"Really, it's nothing." Aubrey's gaze lifted, a shadow in their depths, revealing heaviness there. "I spent the day yesterday having sex with the one and only Carter Hayes. Believe me, I've got nothing to complain about."

Liv examined her. Aubrey was as close as a sister. Regardless of what she'd said, something was wrong. Very wrong. And if Liv guessed, she'd bet Aubrey felt guilty about something. "I'm here, you know that, right? If you need to talk about anything."

Aubrey gave a soft smile, reached across the table and squeezed Liv's hand. "I love you too."

Liv returned the smile, right as a couple walked by. The gentleman wearing a straw hat said to the woman next to him, "We're arriving to port in CocoCay any minute now." Liv couldn't wait to get there. The plan today was to soak in the sun on the beach, drink cocktails, and swim in the ocean on the private island for as long as she could before the ship departed at six o'clock tonight. She'd sent a group text out earlier to tell everyone where she and Miles planned to be for the day in case anyone wanted to join them. She suspected she wouldn't see anyone until dinner tonight, and that was A-okay with her. "So, before we head off, are we going to talk about you and Carter Hayes, and the unbelievable twist of fate that's at work here?"

Aubrey dropped her chin into her hand. "I don't even know if I still believe it. It's like a…"

"Fantasy come true?" Liv offered.

Aubrey snorted a laugh. "Exactly." Then her smiled

faded with her long exhale as she reached for her glass again. "I'm still waiting to wake up and realize I'm dreaming all this."

Now that, Liv understood. She lifted her mimosa to cheers. "You and me both, girl. To this wild adventure."

Aubrey laughed and clanged her glass with Liv's.

LATER THAT AFTERNOON, Miles swam behind Liv on the private island, immensely enjoying the view of her yellow string bikini. The cruise line owned the private island and had built a huge waterpark, but Miles was glad that wasn't Liv's thing. It mostly definitely wasn't his. They'd spent the day soaking up the sun and drinking on the beach. They hit the water after that. Well, after a little nudge from him. The coral reef was bright and beautiful, and Miles hadn't seen color like this in a very long time.

Liv swam farther ahead of him and then suddenly stopped and turned back, pointing right. Miles followed where she directed him, and he gazed upon one of the makeshift plane wrecks. Colorful tropical fish swam around the single engine plane. He gave Liv a thumbs up, and even with the scuba mask, he could see how much she was loving this. He liked her like this. All lit up, without a guard in sight. He'd studied the map of the water before they came to the island, and wanting to see more of that excitement, he took her hand and swam north. There, he pointed at the makeshift shipwreck. Liv's wide eyes met his and he heard her scream of excitement muffled in the water before she swam forward, circling around the shipwreck, looking at it from every angle.

Miles stared after her, not much interested in the ship below. He wondered if this was what love felt like. Bright. Colorful. Easy. Liv turned back to him and waved him forward, calling him over in the direction of the other shipwreck a few feet away. And he followed her, oddly feeling like he'd follow her anywhere, just for more of *this*.

When he reached her, she breached the water and took her snorkel out of her mouth. "How cool was that?"

"Very cool," he said, treading water. "Not so scary in here, is it?"

She laughed softly. "No, it's not so scary. You were right to push me to do this. Thank you for that."

"You're welcome." He grabbed her arm and pulled her in close. "But I don't need to be right."

She licked her lips. "Then what do you need?"

"To see your smile."

And she gave him the exact one he wanted. The same one that had caught his eye when he first saw her at the wedding. A smile that felt handmade just for him.

The thought stayed with him for the remainder of their snorkel, and even after they returned to the cruise ship.

Freshly shaven and showered, Miles checked for his keycard before shoving his wallet into the pocket of his beige slacks that he paired with a white button-down. As he approached the door, he couldn't remember a time he had enjoyed a day this much. He liked being around Liv, near her, touching her, whatever she'd let him do. For years, he'd been searching to fill a void inside him. He'd changed jobs, hoping that would heal the wound. He'd tried to gain more of a personal life, but that had failed to ease the tension in his chest. But slowly, he was beginning to understand why.

Liv.

The magic there. It was…*different.*

Her yellow string bikini had tempted him all day, and she knew it, too, openly teasing him. He had plans for a little retribution on his part, but that would come later. For now, he left his cabin and strode down the hallway, realizing whatever he'd been missing in his life he was finding in Liv.

When he finally reached the main eatery where they served the buffet, he knew food was the last thing he wanted tonight. He hungered for the stunning brunette before him, who stood with her curls free and wild. Liv's skin was sun kissed from their day, and she wore a blouse and skirt, light makeup. "I like this look on you," he told her before dropping a kiss on her cheek.

"What look?" she asked with a sweet smile.

"Fresh. Natural."

She played with one of her curls. "It wasn't on purpose, believe me. I just ran out of time."

He slid his hand on her waist, pulling her in against him. "Then I'm glad you did. Seeing you like this reminds me of you naked." He glanced down into her sparkling eyes. "And I happen to like you that way."

She angled her chin up, offering him so much. "I happen to like that you like me naked."

He chuckled and gladly accepted what she offered, sealing his mouth across hers. When he eventually forced himself to back away, they were both breathless and he considered skipping dinner all together.

But the choice also didn't belong to him. A harsh reminder when her cell phone began to beep and beep and beep.

"That sounds like trouble." She reached into her little purse and took out her cell. She scrolled through then fired off a text before glancing up at Miles. "Well, change of plans, it's just the two of us now."

Miles moved out of the way of the couple passing by them. "Your friends cancelled?"

She nodded and said with a laugh, "They're preoccupied doing other people, which means, we could be doing those things too." She stepped closer, closing the distance, bringing all her warmth and soft curves against him. "How about we get back to that kiss?"

Damn. He was tempted. Too tempted. But he wanted to know her mind as much as he was learning her body. "Let me take you for dinner instead. Somewhere a little nicer than the buffet." Slight disappointment touched her gaze, and he chuckled at that. "I've got plans for us later. Trust me, it'll be worth the wait."

She studied him. Then grinned. "Well, in that case, dinner it is."

He slid her arm in his and he led her down the hallway and up to the top deck. When they entered the Prime Grill, the steak and seafood restaurant, he was glad to find it looked romantic, with a white honeycomb ceiling, black painted walls, and silver and gold accents.

"For two?" the maître d' asked, drawing his attention.

Before he could reply, Liv said, "Yes, please."

"Perfect." The maître d' scooped up two menus. "Right this way."

Miles gestured for Liv to follow and he strode in behind her, his gaze lowering to her incredible ass and the way she put an extra little wiggle to her hips. *Playful, are we?* That bode well for their night ahead. He lifted his attention when they reached the table with a starboard view, and the maître d' set down their menus.

Miles held out Liv's chair, and within minutes, they had a bottle of red wine on the table, two glasses poured.

"I'll have the surf and turf with the lobster tails," Liv said to the brown-haired man, holding the notepad and pen.

"Prime porterhouse," Miles said.

"Perfect." The man smiled. "Enjoy the wine. Your dinner will be out shortly."

As the waiter moved to another table, Miles sat back in his seat. The candlelight on the table cast Liv in a warm glow, somehow making her look softer. Maybe it'd been their time together that had relaxed her guards. Maybe he'd built trust. Whatever it was, he liked how she watched him, openly and eagerly, different than the Liv he'd met at the wedding. The woman who was somewhat closed down. He took a long sip of his wine before asking, "How open are you to answering some personal questions?"

She finished her sip and then laughed softly. "Depends how personal and what you want to know."

Miles knew he treaded dangerous waters, but curiosity got the better of him. "Will you tell me about the guy who hurt you?"

She held his stare, firmly. "How do you know it's a guy and not something else, like a bad childhood?"

He arched an eyebrow at her. "Is it a bad childhood?"

Her mouth twitched and she slowly shook her head.

"No, I actually have amazing parents, who loved me like crazy growing up. Still do." She hesitated, setting her wine glass back on the table. "You really want to hear this? Don't men usually hate hearing about ex's?"

He shrugged. "What's to hate? A past is a past, and it's yours. I'd like to hear about it, if you're willing to share." He wanted to find his way past those guards. First, he needed to understand why they were there.

She let out a long sigh, looking out the window. Her gaze went distant, far away. "It's a boring story."

"Tell me anyway."

Her soft eyes met his again. "His name is Gavin Humphries, the biggest player of all time. I met him through Allie. He's a big time corporate real estate agent. At one time, I wanted to get into that, so Allie thought he was a good connection for me to have. She told me not to go anywhere near him, but Gavin and I...well, we just hit it off. Not that it should have surprised me. He hit it off with every woman. And yet, I thought he actually loved me."

Miles could tell by the tension in her voice where this was going, but he stayed quiet, letting her tell her story. "Within a year, we were engaged, and I thought I'd found the man I'd grow old with." She glanced down at her glass, her chin quivering slightly. She took a long, deep breath and then went on. "You know, it's not that he cheated that gets me."

At the deep pain in her eyes, Miles's jaw set.

"It's that I let myself get that close to someone who I knew could hurt me."

"You can't stop how you feel," Miles offered gently.

She gave a hard nod, lifting her eyes to him again. There was a coldness there. "I thought that way once too. But Gavin taught me that you can stop it. Don't allow something to happen in the first place."

All the little things that Miles needed to know about Liv finally fell into place, and he realized why she was so hesitant to let life fall where it may. Why them living in different states was such a big deal, regardless of the fact that obviously there was something pretty sweet going on between them. She'd let fate lead the way before, and life had burned her.

"What about you?" she asked, obviously wanting the subject changed. "Any bad ex-girlfriends in your past?"

"None that I know of," he said. "I typically don't get close enough for that."

She snatched up her wine glass again, taking a quick sip. "Is there a reason for that?"

"It's nothing complicated. Back in my twenties, my entire focus had been on building my construction company."

"What kind of buildings did you build?"

"Mostly corporate. But the last deal I handled personally was a shopping center."

"Big jobs, then?"

He nodded. "I enjoy the big projects. It stretches the mind."

"Neat." She slowly cocked her head. "Then how did running the nightclub come to be?"

"I realized I wasn't fulfilled, not truly. My personal life suffered greatly from owning the construction company and working long hours, and I needed a change."

"Which is why I guess you haven't had many long-term relationships?"

"Exactly." He stared into her gorgeous eyes, finding it very easy tell her how he felt. "I sold the company to find out what I was missing in life. I've run the club for about a year now...and I'm still looking." *Until I met you*. He didn't feel restless around her. He felt sure, and that was something he'd ever felt before.

She took another big, long sip of her wine, and then cleared her throat. "You must have dated a lot, though? Being you and all."

He chuckled, not sure how to take that. "Being me and all?"

"Yeah, hot and with your...interests," she said with a sweet smile.

He couldn't fight his answering grin. He liked her innocence, probably too much. "Dated, no. Enjoyed sexually, yes. Like I said, I've never met anyone that sparked anything more than a casual encounter." He could see the question in her eyes and answered it for her, taking her hand in his. "Yes, it's different with you. That's exactly why I called for three months trying to come see you. And why I came on this cruise without a second's thought." He felt her hand pull back at the same time her eyes closed off a little. Trying not to scare her, he added, "And that's what this is for me. I'm chasing whatever feels good until I find exactly what I've been missing." To change the topic of conversation from *them*, he asked, "But what about you, Liv? What do you want? Marriage? Children? Is that in the cards for you?"

She nodded. "Yes, I want the husband and the kids, but I'm a lot more of a realist now."

Confused, he arched an eyebrow. "A realist about love?"

"That's right," she said, taking her hand from his to reach for her wineglass again. "It's got to make sense to love one another."

He sat back, regarded her. "Is that you talking or the walls you've built against men like Gavin?"

She stilled, her wine glass halfway to her mouth. "It's not one or the other. There was me before Gavin and me after, walls included. I never make the same mistake twice."

"Not even if the risk was worth it?"

"Not even then." She released a slow breath and set

her wine glass down. "The thing is, for me, it's not about trusting someone again. It's that I knew better. That's what got me, you know. That I knew Gavin was trouble, I knew he was a player, and I let him walk right into my life. I did that to myself. All the heartbreak that came after was my own doing. It took me a good year to crawl out of the depression I sank into after him. I know it seems too logical and hard, even, but it's not that I won't take risks for love. Of course, I would. But love, for me now, has to make sense. Because I know my heart. It can't be bruised that way. I can't take it. And that's a limit I know about me."

Red-hot anger coursed through him and he gave her a slow, understanding nod. To have this woman's heart was a gift. He couldn't imagine mistreating it.

She gave him a funny look. "You think I'm being silly, right?"

"No, Liv, I don't," he told her, controlling the fury licking his veins.

She glanced at her plate a moment then looked up at him through her lashes. "Then what are you thinking?"

He wasn't sure how she'd take what he said next, but he couldn't find a filter. "That if I met Gavin, I'd make sure he regrets what he did to you."

Her eyes widened slightly, and then she gave her sweet laugh. "You know, I think I'd like to see that."

CHAPTER 8

B Y THE TIME dinner was done, and Liv awaited Miles's sexy surprise in the lobby, she knew two things for certain. One, this had been one of her favorite days ever. She'd never enjoyed being in the ocean before, but today had been different. The fish, the bright colors of the coral reef, the shipwrecks, she'd gobbled up every minute of it. She knew with total certainty that having Miles next to her made the ocean less scary. A solid punch from him would no doubt send a shark away. She hadn't had a man in her life for years. She forgot how good it felt. Beyond the fabulous sex, spending time together, laughing, enjoying each other, it all felt...*good*. Really good. And talking about her past didn't hurt like it once did. And she knew both of those things were because of Miles. She wasn't exactly sure what to do about that. She liked him. A lot. She liked how he listened, how, when he talked, he did so with care and compassion. Most of all, she liked the way he lived. Whatever he did, he seemed to do it with everything he had in him, determined to change and keep changing in order to find what satisfied him in life. She remembered a time she was like that, when she had so many dreams. One of those being a corporate real estate agent. She wasn't exactly sure when those dreams went away, but she guessed a lot of it had to do with Gavin. And that just made her mad, not because he cheated, but because she forgot her dreams.

She was lost in those thoughts when Miles's surprise plan for the night became clear after she'd been handed a piece of paper by one of the entertainment workers. She studied the paper then looked up at Miles. "A sexy scavenger hunt?"

"Surprised?" he asked with a sly smile.

"Uh, yeah." Of all the *plans* that Liv thought Miles might have, this had most definitely not been what she thought. Standing with two dozen couples in the main lobby, she examined the *insane* list in her hands.

To be done in order:

1. *Give your bra to someone on the dance floor.*
2. *Get a spanking in public on the pool deck.*
3. *Ask a man to autograph your cleavage at the piano bar.*
4. *Go to the bow of the ship and have someone talk dirty to you.*
5. *Get a condom from someone at the stern of the ship.*

She took in each and every word and then she slowly

lifted her head to Miles. "I'm so confused right now," she admitted. Where was the sex? The dirty times that his eyes had promised her?

Miles gave her that panty-melting grin. "Stop thinking and just go with it." The world faded away when he took a step closer, captured her chin, and brought his powerful gaze down to her eye level. "Let me be clear, Liv, the only guy doing anything on this list to you is me. Understood?"

At that firm command in his voice, she shivered. "I understand that when you look at me like that and talk in that deep, sexy voice that I want to rip your clothes off, yes."

His eyes softened with his chuckle. "And the rules, you get those too?"

"Yeah, yeah," she said, "but, are you not coming on this scavenger hunt with me?"

"I'll find you on it."

Before she could reply, Alfonzo, the man who'd organized the body shots, said, "All right, friends, are we ready? Complete all the items and whichever person comes back first wins a bottle of tequila."

Loud applause filled the lobby, echoing in the grand space. Liv slid Miles a look, spotting the slight curve of his mouth. Oh, yeah, he knew she was watching him. Obviously, he was changing up the game to suit him, and she decided to listen to him and go with it. So far anything he did proved hot as hell and ended with a mind-blowing orgasm.

Alfonzo lifted a hand in the air and called, "Ready, set, go."

"Let the games begin," Miles said, yanking her forward and gave her a searing kiss and then he smacked her ass. "You better get running. Don't want to lose, after all!"

She spun away feeling the laughter bubble up. Okay, so maybe this wasn't going to be so bad after all. She followed the other participants as they moved through the hallway down to the party room where the DJ had electronic music blasting through the speakers. The dance floor was already jam packed. The others in the game began taking off their bras to give to someone. Liv scanned the club but couldn't find Miles anywhere. With a sigh, she reached up the back of her shirt, right as two hands gripped her arms. In less time it took to blink, she was spun around and brought up against a post. Miles's hands braced her face, his mouth sealing against hers. He ravaged her with kisses. He melted her damn insides, turning her into hot, fiery liquid that was his to drink. His tongue devilishly stroked hers and their lips moved in sync. His hands were everywhere, squeezing, kneading, waking every single inch of her up until there was no music. No people. Only them, and this wild place he took her.

Just as she became desperate for more, he was gone.

She slowly opened her eyes, feeling wet, hot, and needy as she glanced down, realizing he'd stolen her bra. She blinked, finding people watching her, one lady was fanning herself. Her face burned from Miles, but surprisingly not from embarrassment. She'd never thought being watched would get her off like it did, but she liked that feeling of having eyes on her. The eroticism of it all. The proof that she was sexy and young and wild.

Ready to find Miles again, Liv rushed forward, remembering she had a list to follow. She couldn't find any of the other participants, so she hurried out to the hallway, and then out onto the pool deck. The bar, as always, was alive with partygoers. Her face flushed hot at the thought that he'd spank her in front of all these people. Nervous excitement fluttered in her belly.

Laughter came from her left. She spotted one of the women getting spanked by a half-naked cowboy. It occurred to her then that that's not what Liv wanted. She didn't want silliness. She wanted a passionate man to hold her, to command her, to take what he wanted and to give her the same.

Goosebumps suddenly rose on her flesh as a hard body closed in behind her. Miles's hand slid up her back until his fingers threaded in her hair. "A little pain always does make things more interesting." His low voice rumbled over her, taking her far away from there. He fisted her hair, nudging her head to the side while he kissed her neck, turning her bones to mush. Her eyes fluttered shut at the sheer force of him as he stepped to the side, the strength of his body right there. She fell into him, into the safe feeling he provided. He cupped her bottom. Squeezed twice. Then blasted a hard swat against her butt cheek. Heat flooded her. She leaned back, not ashamed to want that feeling again. *More.*

He slapped again. And again. And again.

The air got thick. She felt dizzy with the desire coursing through her.

But then all that strength behind her was gone.

She snapped her eyes open and spun around, the world shaky beneath her, until her vision cleared. Every set of eyes on her prickled against her flesh, making even the breeze on her arms tickle in a good way. But then she found Miles. His heated smile widened before he faded into the crowd.

Drenched with desire and encouraged by the envy she spotted in more than a few women's faces, she moved back the way she came, having a hard time remembering where the piano bar even was, or if she even still had legs. Her panties were soaked, her limbs nearly numb. She went right down the hallway. When suddenly, she realized she should've gone left. "Dammit." She turned around, nearly walking right into someone. "Sorry."

The man reached out for her. "Are you all right?"

"Yes, thank you," she breathed, trying to find her working body parts.

She headed the opposite direction until she saw the large crystal chandelier hanging in the center of the classy bar, decorated in red and black accents and more mirrors than she could possibly count.

Just as she approached bar, a hand caught hers. The room spun as she was snatched away and pulled behind a large pillar. "Stay right here," Miles ordered, a firm look in his eyes now. One that made her belly tighten. This man looking at her now was the *Dominant*. The man he'd obviously contained. "Move an inch and security cameras will see what I'm about to do."

Before she could even question him, or make sense out of how wildly hot his dominance made her, he grabbed the front of her dress and exposed her breasts. Anyone could have seen them, watched this. Her breath caught somewhere deep in her throat, excitement coursing red-hot in her veins, secretly wanting for just that to happen. He cupped her breasts, sucked each one, bit each nipple, and she unabashedly ground herself against him, lacing her fingers into his hair, holding him there, wanting him *there*. She was a panting mess when he tried to lean away. She held on, and he nipped hard at her breast. *Hard.* She somehow gasped and shuddered all the same. "Don't ruin my fun now," he said with a dark, devilish grin. "You've got two more tasks ahead of you." He grabbed a marker from his back pocket, took the top off with his teeth and then signed Miles onto her breast. She wasn't sure why, but having his name on her like this felt like the most erotic thing she'd ever experienced. She felt marked by *him* in the best possibly way.

His sly grin was the last thing she saw as he headed down the hallway. She peeled herself off the wall, trying desperately to catch her breath, wondering how in the hell she was going to make it to the last item. Her panties were soaking wet, her sex throbbing for his touch…his cock, and when she looked at the next item, she whimpered.

The walk to the bow of the ship felt long, but did nothing to ease the tension coiled tight inside her. When she finally made it outside, the light breeze brushed across her, doing nothing to cut through the heat blazing between her thighs. People were everywhere, laughing, talking, but her full attention went to Miles. He leaned against the railing, soft lights along the ground guided her to him. He was magnificent. His grin haughty, yet warm. His eyes dark and stern, yet passion burned in their depths. Her heart raced with each and every step she took toward him. She thought he'd grab her, spin her around, and quietly talk dirty in her ear.

That's not what happened.

He cupped her face, confidently looking her right in

the eyes. "Tonight we've played a game, but what will happen next is no game, Liv." He yanked her up against him and then murmured in her ear, "Tonight you will spread your legs for me, and I will fuck you until all you can do is scream my name. And after you come you will say: 'Thank you, Sir'. Because tonight, you're *mine*…completely, and this will please me."

Overwhelmed by his sheer presence, her breath caught somewhere deep in her throat. Her body hummed with the passion he put out in the world. Her pussy pulsed in need. "Miles," she barely managed.

"One more task," he said firmly. "Go. Now."

She turned away from him, even though it was the exact opposite of what she wanted to do. Her legs shook, almost like she hung right there ready to climax, as she somehow walked down the hallway, only one thing on her mind. Miles's hard body thrusting inside her, until they both broke apart.

On her way down the hallway, toward the stern of the ship, she passed Miles's cabin door, when suddenly it swung open. He snatched her by the waist and yanked her inside before he slammed her against the door. "You remember the rules for tonight, Liv?"

"Yes," she gasped.

"Good girl." He ripped off her panties and the fabric burned against her flesh. Then he had her skirt lifted, her legs around his waist and he was driving himself inside her. "Give me what I want, Liv."

And she did. She screamed his name, not because he asked, but because she had no choice. No say whatsoever in how her body responded. He'd taken control of it all. His masculine growls filled her ears, his strength and power brushed across her senses, as he pounded lust and pleasure into her, until he was thrusting harder, faster, and she was going to a place she'd never been. One that had no beginning and no end. The place only he could take her. Pure freedom. And only when he got her there, did he follow her.

She vaguely felt his cock pulsating inside her when he said, "The rules were clear, Liv."

She didn't need another reminder. The words fell easily from her lips. "Thank you, Sir."

He dropped a sweet, soft kiss on her lips that was a stark contrast to how he'd taken her a moment ago, and whispered against her lips, "Now doesn't that sound pretty."

CHAPTER 9

THE NEXT MORNING, the ship docked in Nassau, Bahamas at a little after seven o'clock in the morning, unbeknownst to Miles as he slept. He awoke to find Liv already gone from his bed to meet up with her friends, and before hopping in the shower, he ordered room service. Out on the balcony with his breakfast, the heat of the day had already set in and he stared upon the vast blue water. He was beginning to feel terrible for taking up all of Liv's time on their reunion cruise, but he knew without a doubt that if the roles were reversed, his friends would understand too. And he was not ready to give up the hours he got with her. He'd come on this cruise for answers, and he was beginning to get them. He loved being with her. He liked how she made him feel. Content...*happy.* Whatever this was going on with them, his feelings for her weren't dulling, they were only intensifying.

Lost in his thoughts, he stayed on the balcony for the better part of the morning, until he'd received Liv's text to meet him in the lobby. When he spotted her approaching, she wore a summer dress over her bikini. The sun looked good on her. Each day her tan got a bit darker. He liked how her freckles were coming out on her nose. She had her hair up, bringing all his attention to her long gorgeous neck, making him reconsider his plans to leave the ship today. "All squared away with your friends?" he asked when she reached him.

"I actually couldn't find anyone," she said, giving a cute grin. "Apparently, they're having as much fun as I am on this cruise."

"Is that so," he murmured, sliding his hand across her lower back and pulling all her soft curves against him. "I guess that means I get you all to myself today, hmm?"

She tilted her chin up, offering him so much with those sweet eyes. "Seems so."

Consumed by this magical thing between them, he took what she wanted him to have and dropped a soft kiss onto her lips, a tease of what was to come today.

"But it works for us," she said, when he leaned away. "That's kind of how our friendship has always been. We're there for each other when it matters, but our lives have always seemed to take us all in opposite directions."

"Sounds like good friends to me," he said.

She agreed with a nod.

Miles took her hand and liked how that felt. Natural. Right. For years, he'd spent his life alone. But *this*...yeah, he liked this. "I've got a surprise for us today," he told her.

"Oh," she said, stepping back a little. "You made plans already?"

He noted the disappointment in her expression. "Plans that can be easily changed or cancelled, if need be. Did you already have something in mind?"

She nibbled her lip, shifting from side-to-side. "Well, there was something that I really want to do while in Nassau. It won't take long. Can your surprise wait an hour or two?"

"Of course," he said. "Where are we off to?"

At that question, she led them to a local pet store twenty minutes away in a cab. Curious, Miles stayed quiet, watching Liv study each and every item she picked up, from toys to beds. She also studied the price tag. Wanting to understand her, he asked, "Have you always been such an animal lover?"

"Always," she explained, moving down another aisle. "I've got a cat at home. His name is Fritz. I really want a dog, but with how much time I spend at work, it would just be unfair."

Miles took the mental note. "You work long hours?"

"Incredibly long." Regret was heavy in her voice. "But that's because Allie's growing her company. We've just been so busy this last year."

"And you like that?" Miles asked behind her, as she

placed a couple cat toys in the cart.

"Working so much, you mean?" She glanced over her shoulder at him.

He nodded.

"Not really, but Allie needs me, and I know it's temporary. She wants to grow just a little more before she can hire more staff. Things should settle down after that, and maybe my doggy dreams will happen then."

Something about that sat wrong in Miles's gut. "Seems unfair not to have what you want in life, simply to make someone else happy."

Her eyebrows rose. "So, what are you suggesting I do? Leave Allie when she needs me most? That seems harsh."

He considered that and shrugged. "Only harsh to her, if she doesn't love you like you love her. From my time spent with Allie, I'd think she'd want you to be happy."

"Of course she would, but I'd feel terrible for leaving her when things are so hectic."

Miles arched a brow. "Have they ever not been hectic?" He knew what a growing company took. It never calmed down, only got worse and busier until the funds were there to hire the staff.

She quickly glanced away. "It'll calm down. Soon. I'm not worried about that."

Liv stayed quiet while she stopped in front of the cat

food and began piling cans and bags in the cart. He didn't want to push, even if he thought her dreams mattered as much as Allie's did, so he changed the subject. "Are you expecting to find a pack of strays somewhere?" he asked with a soft laugh.

When she moved onto the bigger bags of cat food, he gently nudged her out of the way and began sliding them into the bottom of the cart as she explained, "When Hurricane Dorian hit, the local animal shelter was destroyed, and over one hundred animals died. But thankfully, over two hundred animals were shipped to shelters in the US." She looked back and smiled warmly. "That's how I got Fritz. He was one of the cats that survived the hurricane, so I made a promise to myself that if I ever came to Nassau, I'd show the shelter some love for all the love that Fritz has given me."

He added another bag to her cart. "So that's what you're doing here? Buying things for the shelter?"

When he straightened, she nodded at him. "Whenever I travel, I always go to shelters and bring stuff. I wish I could save more animals, but I do what I can."

Hell, this woman was sweet. Kind in ways he'd never really seen before. She loved hard, not only her friends, but her family, and now it seemed, animals too. He thought Liv had a lot going for her, but this warm heart she had, he liked that most.

She grabbed a couple cans of wet food then turned

back to him. "Do you have any pets?"

He shook his head. "My mother wasn't a fan of animals. She has a phobia of cats, so we never had any animals growing up."

Liv looked horrified at his admission. "Well, you need to change that. Believe me, animals make us better people. And the love they give…" She went all soft and warm. "There is no better love than that."

Miles doubted that. He bet her love felt pretty damn good. A tightness in his chest eased that he hadn't realized had been there, making his breath slow and easy. And it was this exact feeling that he'd been chasing ever since his first night with Liv. He was beginning to see her nurturing side, and it occurred to him then that this was what was missing in his life… he'd certainly never experienced it growing up. His mother had been cold, aloof. His father worked all the time, never thinking it was his job to parent, while Miles found a family with his friends. This warm touch of a loving woman was nothing he'd known before.

He broke away from his thoughts when she suddenly laughed softly. "Why are you looking at me like that?"

"Come here." He snatched her hand and brought her soft curves against his hard plains. Everything felt right when he lowered his mouth to hers, and kissed her hard, passionately, until she melted against him. Only when she softened enough, telling him he'd kissed her like she deserved, did he back away. "You're a good woman, Liv Sloane. This world is lucky place to have you in it. And I'm a lucky man to be with you now."

She gave him a smile that had him all wrapped up. "Well…thank you. I feel lucky to be here with you too."

He kissed her again. This time, all for himself. For years he'd searched, trying to understand what was missing in his life, in his soul, and for the first time ever, he finally felt like that question had been answered. When he backed away, her eyes slowly opened, revealing her dark pupils. "Wait here," he told her with a grin.

"Where are you going?" she called after him.

He fetched two more carts and then returned to her. "Let's see what else those animals at the shelter need." Her brow furrowed a little in obvious confusion, and he set to clear that up. "Surely, I can't let you do all this charity work and stand by doing nothing. I've got money. Let me support your cause."

Her eyes widened. "Really?"

He gave a firm nod. "You're right. This is a good thing to do. Those beds you were looking at before, would the animals like those?" Her eyes softened then, and she threw herself at him.

"Thank you," she whispered in his ear.

His chest took a direct hit, filling with unfamiliar warmth. Yeah, *this* he could get used to.

LATER THAT AFTERNOON, after delivering all of the pet supplies to the shelter and spending time with the animals there, Miles's plan for the day took over. They'd taken a taxi back to the beach, and a speedboat took them to a private island, where they'd spent the day soaking up the sun. Liv stretched out on the beach bed, its white curtains waving in the wind. They weren't alone on the island. Beds lined the coast, but the only noise reaching them was the waves washing up on shore. Miles hadn't left a single detail out of their excursion today, and in between swimming and hiking through the private island's jungle trail, Liv couldn't quite remember a day she enjoyed more. And the hot-as-hell guy lying next to her, with his eyes closed, was the reason. Liv wasn't exactly sure when it happened, but the part of her heart that said Miles was all wrong for her began to grow quiet. He was a great guy. Sweet and attentive. Dominant and powerful. Everything she ever hoped she'd find in a man and more. Everyday he'd put the effort in to make their moments together special.

She studied him next to her. This confident man who never seemed to fill the silence with small talk. She'd never felt so comfortable with anyone. At every turn, he surprised her, filling her nights with adventure, passion, and making her smile more than she could remember in a long time. All she kept asking herself was: Why had she shut him down so fiercely these past three months? Because of the distance between them? Because she told herself she'd never date a guy who was both charming and edgy? It began to feel like her reasons for staying away were more like excuses. And she wasn't sure how she felt about that. Pathetic that she'd given up on believing anything was possible? Embarrassed that fear ruled her life? Sad that she shut down a chance at happiness?

Miles's eyes were still closed, but the side of his mouth curved. "What's on your mind?"

She felt the urge to explain, but also was drowned in fear of what he'd say back. Instead, she said the next best truth, "I feel terrible that I can't think of one magical thing to do for you to make this trip as incredible as you've made mine."

He turned his head, sliding his sunglasses down his nose, revealing his potent gaze. "Believe me, you've made my trip incredible. It's the spark I needed."

She flipped on her side, leaning her head against her hand. "What do you mean? The spark?"

He mirrored her movement, shifting onto his side, taking his sunglasses fully off. That potent stare held hers for a beat, obviously choosing his words carefully. "I'm not sure how to explain what I mean, other than to say that my life feels stagnant, and it's not a position I enjoy."

She couldn't help but admire the golden tone of his skin, the stretching and flexing of his muscles, but she forced herself to stay focused, curious about him. "Stagnant in what way?"

A long slow breath passed through his mouth. "I wake up and it feels like I'm living the exact same day. Ever feel like that?"

She gazed into his piercing stare, overwhelmed by him, of how easy it was for him to speak his truth. "I wouldn't say my life has ever felt stagnant, but I know how it feels to be stuck in a little bit of Groundhog Day scenery myself."

His bicep flexed, the veins bulging there, as he rested his head on his hand. "In what way?"

She cleared her throat, focusing on the conversation. *Again.* "I've just…" The words were going to come out so easily, but then her voice caught. Admitting deeper parts of herself had landed her on dangerous ground before, but she suddenly found she wanted Miles to know her. "I actually have been living the same day, over and over again, and it's not the day I thought I'd be living."

Of course, he didn't miss what she wasn't saying between the lines. "What did you think it'd be, then?"

"I thought I'd be a commercial real estate agent. I mean, that had been the plan. I'd finished college and everything. All I needed to do was get my real estate license."

"Then what happened?"

"Life happened," she said with a sigh. "After college, I wanted some real-life experience and saw Allie's job posting. She hired me, and then a friendship grew between us. One of those crazy friendships that feels kinda soul deep, you know?" He nodded, fully understanding, and she added, "After that, I just never left. She pays me nearly as much as I'd make on my own, and I am happy working there, alongside her, even if it's not exactly what I thought I'd be doing."

Miles hesitated. "But you're not satisfied?"

She considered that then lifted a shoulder. "I hadn't really thought about it too much, and I guess I'm not totally satisfied with my life. But I mean, is anyone?"

"Yes," Miles stated. "Some people are, just not us, apparently."

She laughed softly. "So what are you going to do after the cruise to make your life less stagnant?"

His fingers froze on her thigh, heady gaze meeting hers. "That depends."

"On?"

"On what happens after the cruise ends," he said boldly. She was flattered by how sure he seemed about her, but felt the same strangling fear creep up. He went on before she could address it. "Something's been missing in my life. I've known that for a very long time. I'm tired of not finding out what that is and going after it."

"I envy that about you," she said honestly. "I wish I was bold and brave like that."

"You are," he said. "I'd say since I met you you've been pretty damn bold and brave."

She laughed softly. "But that's different."

"Why?"

"It's fun."

He nodded. "I suspect that's what life should be about."

She caught the darkness in his gaze. "But your life hasn't been fun?"

"Like I said, a spark has been missing. I've felt that spark on this trip. It's not boring. Not full of responsibility. It's…refreshing."

She watched him closely. "Okay, well, I guess that does make me feel better, at least you're getting something good out of this too."

"I am," he said firmly. "So, stop worrying about me, all right?"

"Okay, I won't." She laughed then slid closer, moving against him, resting her head on his shoulder. She pondered all he'd said. "When, and how did you realize you needed a change in your life?"

His tender touch began its trail over her hip, warming all the spots he grazed. "It wasn't something that happened overnight. I was very content. My construction company satisfied me professionally. My personal life was where I wanted to be. I very much liked being alone. Unattached."

"Then what happened?"

He laughed, which softened his typically intense eyes. "All of my very single friends got married and started having children. Being around them…well, it changed me."

"It made you want that?"

"Not want necessarily, but it showed me a different kind of world."

She felt the weight of his words, the darkness there too. "It was hard for you growing up?"

His gaze went distant, far away from them. "Hard for me, no. But it hardened me, yes. My mother is a cold woman. Not horrible in any means, just cold. I was raised by nannies, who quit often. My mother and I are not close and talk only a few times a year."

"And your father?"

"I feel closer to the man who bought my company off me than I do my father."

She swallowed deeply, suddenly realizing why Miles put in so much effort in trying to come see her, where other men would have given up. It didn't take much to realize he hadn't felt much for any women, and he liked her. She liked him too. And maybe...*just maybe*...he'd never felt that before. "Well, I think it's great that you're on this new adventure, searching for what makes you happy."

He gave her a sweet smile, brushed his knuckles across her cheek. "Do you?"

She gave a firm nod. "You deserve all the happiness, Miles. Truly." And she meant that.

Something crossed his expression then. Something warm and addictive and something that could swallow a woman up whole, making her forget the world could be a hard place. He leaned up, hovering over her, and before he kissed her, he said, "I'm not the only one, Liv."

CHAPTER 10

T WO DAYS HAD flown by. Too damn fast. There were no more ports to stop at, no more adventures, only open sea for the last two days and the awareness that Miles's time with Liv was running out. Change come on the final days of the cruise, and not only for Miles and Liv. Two of Liv's friends jumped ship. Kendall had a family emergency, and Aubrey had decided not to come back aboard the cruise before departing Nassau. Miles felt like doing the same damn thing. The next stage of his life would be decided soon, and he felt the weight of that sitting heavy on his chest.

Either he'd stick around in Vegas a little longer, with the intent of going back and forth to California getting to know Liv better, or he'd leave for his next adventure to find the *thing* that was missing from his life. Even now, as he guided Liv across the dancefloor on their final night of this adventure, his lips brushing across her neck, she felt like the missing piece. He sensed this the day he met her, and he sensed it now too. He barely understood it, and such a thing seemed impossible to explain to a woman who refused to let fate guide her way.

Conflicted on where to go from here, he placed a final kiss on the sweet spot on her neck, loving the way she leaned into him. The slow, instrumental music in the ballroom came from the four-piece band on the stage. Large crystal chandeliers hung over the wooden, oval dancefloor surrounded by tables covered in black linens. While the room was elegant, Liv was all Miles could see now.

She cocked her head, laughed softly. "You're looking at me funny. What is it?"

His chest tightened. He'd been careful so far, not wanting to push too hard, too fast. Not wanting to come on too strong, hoping, praying even, that she'd see this thing between them was magical and rare and something they needed to chase. But tomorrow was coming up quick. "I wish we had longer," he told her. "I don't want this…*us*…to end."

He expected her to shut him down. But she surprised him. "I wish we had longer too," she whispered.

His feet stopped moving, the air nearly gone from his lungs. "I admit, I wasn't expecting that answer."

He began dancing again, moving them slowly, needing to see every emotion crossing her face.

"I admit I wasn't expecting to say it." Her cheeks began losing a little of their color, her hand becoming clammy in his. "But now it's out there, and I don't really know what to do with that."

It seemed simple to him. "Probably be happy we've found something pretty great."

Darkness settled over her face, hardness too. "Or have we just made things even more impossible than they were before?"

The others in the room faded away. His entire world narrowing on her. "How can this be impossible, Liv? This is good between us. So damn good. Nothing is impossible."

She held his stare for a long time. "I really don't understand how you're so sure about…well, *me*. About us. Why are you so invested in seeing where this goes?"

Heat touched her gaze when he leaned in and claimed her mouth, passionately kissing her, putting all of what he felt, what couldn't possibly be explained, into the kiss. "Because of *that*," he murmured, brushing his lips across hers. "That feeling. That spark. I don't need months to date you to know that there is something incredible here. I knew this thing between us was different the day I met you."

He saw the flicker of emotion in her eyes, the tears welling there before she tore her hand from his and stepped back. "I…I need some air." Then she was gone, her slinky black satin dress swirling around her as she headed for the deck.

He had no choice but to follow. The same instincts

that drove him to come on this cruise drove him now. She entranced him, commanded him in a way no one had before her, and he doubted any woman would after her. Even in this moment, the bare skin exposed by the dress's low cut back called for his mouth, his kiss.

Mine echoed in his soul.

Once outside, the soft lighting illuminated her in the dark night as she moved to the railing at the bow of the ship. Her deep breaths were visible as she stared out to the dark water, her shoulders rising and falling as the strands of hair that escaped her bun fluttered in the breeze.

He closed the distance and when she leaned back against him, he knew pushing now was the right thing to do. He dropped a kiss on her shoulder. "Tell me what you're thinking."

She turned. The tears in her eyes felt like a punch to the throat. "You have to understand that I promised myself I would never let this happen again. I swore to myself that I wouldn't ever date someone when it doesn't make sense. I know you think that is silly. I know *everyone* thinks that is silly. That I need to get over my hang-ups. But I know myself, and I remember the feeling of wanting to die, of not seeing the joy in anything, of forgetting I'm special and important without a man." Her voice blistered, her hair fluttering around her face in the breeze. "Gavin broke me, Miles. Broke me until I was nothing. I can't be broken again."

Fuck, he'd destroy Gavin if he met him. Miles's grip tightened, wanting desperately to protect her. He cupped her face. "I don't think you're silly, Liv. You're scared, and rightfully so. But I would never break you."

A tear slid down her face. "That's not something you can promise. Neither of us can. No matter how much I like you, our lives are states apart. That's the reality here. I can't move. Do you understand that? My mother needs me. Even if we made this long-distance thing work and then decided to get married, I can never move for you. Ever, Miles. You'll have to leave your life behind in Vegas, and how is that fair?"

"Because that's my choice, Liv, and I'd make it."

She heaved a long sigh. "Of course, you can say that now, but will it be so easy when the time actually comes to do it?"

He looked her dead in the eye. "Yes, it will, because I'm not talking about moving later. I'll move now."

Her eyes widened. Lips parted then shut. "You can't possibly mean that."

He slid his hand into her hair, feeling the connection with her that locked him in tight. "But I do."

"But your friends and the club," she countered. "You even said it yourself. They're your found family. How could I ask you to leave them behind?"

He pinned her between the railing and his body,

caging what he so desperately wanted to hold onto. "You wouldn't be asking. I'm offering. Dmitri can easily find someone to run the nightclub. And my friends would understand."

She hesitated. "You'll get bored of me."

He couldn't stop the chuckle that escaped him. "How could I possibly get bored of you?"

"I don't usually have wild sex. I can't be the submissive you need."

"Of course, I understand why that scares you." He tucked the fallen strands of her hair behind her ear. "But it's impossible that I would grow bored of you, and like I said before, I wanted this chance to see if our connection stalled or grew. And for me, it grew. These days with you have been amazing. I want more time together."

The doubt slowly left her face. "You'd do that? Move to San Francisco just to see where we end up. Just like that?"

He gave a firm nod. "For *this*...for us to see where this goes...yeah, Liv, just like that." He cupped her cheek again, laying it all on the line now. "I know you're scared to take a risk. I understand why, and if my moving to San Francisco helps you shed those fears, then I'll move. It's that simple, Liv. I want this. I want you."

Tears filled her eyes, her voice nearly inaudible, as she cupped her face. "Miles..." And then she did what he least expected.

Her lips met his, and he couldn't think after that, couldn't do anything but grab her legs as she wrapped them around his waist. Her kiss felt raw, the guards she'd had in place were *gone*. She gripped his shirt, holding him to her. "I need you, Liv," he said, breaking off the kiss.

Her hooded eyes met his, so rich with emotion. "I need you too."

The words echoed through him the entire way back to his cabin. The moment he had her alone, he slid his fingers through the straps of her dress until the flimsy fabric brushed over her bare nipples and fell to the floor. She wore little black panties which he went down on one knee to remove. He kissed her thigh, and he knew just what she wanted when her hands slid through his hair. And as he leaned in, smelling her, drawing her sweet scent in deep, he knew what was on the line. One misstep with her and everything would unravel. He felt the tension ripple through him. Her heart had been too bruised, too battered, and he realized the responsibility of that. The trust she needed. "I won't hurt you, Liv," he promised, glancing up her eager body.

"Please…" Deep emotion flashed in her eyes as she guided him toward her sex.

His tongue met soft, hot flesh, and she quivered, a soft moan spilling from her mouth as he gently tongued her heat. He played, and teased, until those moans grew louder. When he dipped lower, tasting all of her, urgency filled him.

She tasted like *his*. Eventually, he kissed his way back up her body and took one taut nipple into his mouth and pinched the other hard. She hissed beautifully and he grinned, tonguing the saltiness off her flesh and then made his way back to her mouth. She was a hot, boneless mess when he cupped her ass, bringing all her warm flesh against his clothed hard body. "Go to the bed," he told her, leaning away. "Get on your knees for me."

He watched as she did as he asked. In seconds, he shed his clothes and applied a condom.

The softness of her curves drew him forward to stand behind her. This woman who changed so much this week had him hard and ready, wanting everything from her. And then wanting it again. And again. Heat and tension filled him as he covered her with his body, claiming what had felt like his from the moment he set his eyes on her. He liked her here, protected. Safe from the fucked-up world that hurt her. Desperate to have more of her, he slid a hand down to her sex, sliding his fingers through her soaking wet folds before he worked her clit in slow circles. Her moans echoed around him, telling him just what she wanted. "I'll give you everything you need. Anything you want." He held his hard cock in one hand and her hip in the other and then he entered her. Slowly. She took every inch, and he wanted her to feel those inches. To feel all of him.

He brought her back to his chest, holding him to her. Protected. Nothing could touch her here, while he rocked his hips, hard and fast. She felt handmade just for him, her body hugging his perfectly with every stroke. Her moans the sweetest sound he'd ever heard, driving him wild all the same.

Soon her body submitted to the desire he fed. Her fingernails dug into his thighs, her body became ridged, before she exploded with a scream and a hard shudder. Locked in his embrace, the power of his climax stormed over him. But another need took over, a primal one, a feeling more powerful than anything he'd ever felt before. "You're mine," he growled in her ear, loving the answering moan she gave. "All mine, Liv."

CHAPTER 11

THE CLOCK ON the nightstand glowed one o'clock in the morning when Liv jolted awake. She glanced over her shoulder, finding Miles wasn't in bed with her. She sat up, taking stock. The cabin was quiet as she lay naked in the bed. She was sore in all the right places. But raw in others. These days with Miles were magical, special in ways she never would have believed possible. She felt entirely different now than she had when she'd stepped on this cruise. She'd come to give herself a break from her life. Now she realized maybe it wasn't a break she needed, but a complete change. She envied that about Miles so much. How he was willing to pick up and move to go after what he wanted all because it felt right. For so long, she'd been afraid to trust herself and her judgment, thinking that she'd always get everything wrong. Truth was, she didn't want to be afraid anymore. She wanted to be this exciting new woman who went after adventures and things that made her happy. Why couldn't this be her life? Wild and free and…*happy*.

The light in the bathroom was turned off, but the

balcony door was open, and laughter came from the other side. Curious, she slid out of bed, careful to stay quiet, and moved closer to the door when she caught an unfamiliar feminine voice.

"We can't wait for you to come home," the woman said. "The nightclub has been…well, they need you," she said with a soft laugh. "And the dungeon just isn't the same without you there."

"I'll be home before you know it," Miles replied, his voice sounding sleepy and deep. Incredibly sexy. "And not to worry, we'll get the nightclub back in shape."

But the nightclub was fine without him, at least that's how Miles had made it seem. They didn't need him, he had said.

Liv reeled at the thought, as a woman said, "I've got no doubt you will. So enough about that, how about we stop talking about us and start talking about you and Liv? Tell me every single adventure you've had. All the details. I need to live vicariously through you."

Miles chuckled softly, and then he began explaining everything they'd done on their trip, finishing up with the Sexy Scavenger Hunt. Of course, he skimmed over the details without spilling all their secrets.

"A sexy scavenger hunt," a man said, his voice full of intrigue. "We should do something of that sort in the dungeon. The members would like that."

"I'm in," the woman said. Her voice lost some of its

heat as she added, obviously to Miles, "It sounds like things are going well with Liv then."

Liv could almost see his nod as he replied, "We're moving in the right direction. Everywhere we've stopped has been romantic and beautiful. It's very easy to get swept away in the moment."

Liv felt her throat tighten. Her heart slowly began to speed up. It *was* easy to get lost, and she suddenly realized just how easily she'd been swept away. All of this had been a magical fantasy she never wanted to wake up from. But she'd seen the other side of when fate led the way, the painful parts. The parts that crushed her so she didn't even look like herself anymore.

"So, then, this Liv really *is* as special as you thought?" the woman asked.

This time, Miles didn't hesitate. "More so than I could have even imagined."

"Amazing news," a man said. "Any talk on what will happen tomorrow?"

Liv couldn't stand it any longer. She peeked around the curtain. Miles had his back to her, with his ankles resting up on the railing. A quick look at the phone and Liv recognized them as Dmitri and his wife Presley, who she'd met at the wedding.

She moved away quickly to remain unseen as Miles replied, "We've chatted a little bit, but nothing is set in stone."

The world spun around Liv as Miles added gently, "She's been hurt before and is very logical about all this. The long-distance thing is a problem, and I'm well aware of that."

Presley snorted. "Just because you live in two different states doesn't mean you can't make it work. People do it all the time. You can go visit her on the weekends, or she can come see us. Totally doable."

Miles paused like he was choosing his words carefully. "I've offered to move to San Francisco."

Stunned silence sank into the darkness. The type of silence that instantly made Liv go ice cold.

Even Liv felt the weight of Dmitri's shock when he asked, "You are that sure about her?"

Miles let out a long slow breath. "What I feel for her hasn't dulled. If anything, it's more intense now than before. I'd be a damn fool not to see where we end up."

"But you'd be moving away from all of us," Presley said, tears in her voice. "Your job. Your family here. We all need you, Miles."

"Presley," Dmitri said firmly.

"Well, it's true," she said, her voice quivering.

"I know this is hard, Presley," Miles murmured. "I haven't made this decision lightly."

Liv shut her eyes, barely able to breathe. No, no. no. This wasn't supposed to be like this. He made it seem easy. That moving to San Fran was the right thing to do.

But how was *this* the right thing?

Presley sniffed and asked, "Why can't she move to Vegas?"

"Liv's very close to her family. Her mother has MS. Obviously, leaving her would be hard, and I won't ask her to." He hesitated. "Like I said, she's been hurt before. Trusting anyone is understandably hard, and to see where this goes, I need to take this leap of faith to show her I'm all in."

The room began to swallow Liv up. He said his friends would understand. That he'd been searching for something missing in his life. How was this good for anyone? His friends would miss him. He was needed at the club. They had no idea if this could work between them. If she could even *be* what he needed. He was a Dominant at a sex club. Sure, she'd had fun, but she wasn't sure she could go up on a stage like that woman or kneel at his feet.

He'll grow bored of you, a dark voice echoed in her head. *He'll look elsewhere when that happens.*

"I'm really happy for you, Miles," Presley said, her voice crackling. "But it won't be the same without you here. With us. Where you belong."

"It'll be all right," Miles said tenderly. "I'll visit often enough. You won't even know I'm gone."

"Now *that* would be impossible," Dmitri said, his voice thick with the affection of an obviously close friendship. "Your absence will be greatly felt by all."

Liv shut her eyes and breathed against the swelling of her heart. He'd leave them, his found family and life for *her.* For what? Because fate put two people together who had a connection—a magical one, yes—but was it real? Could it be? Or was this all a fantasy that was always meant to end?

Breaking into her thoughts, Miles said, "We'll talk soon."

"Goodnight, Miles," Dmitri replied.

The silence indicated the video chat ended, and Miles' long exhale cut through the darkness. Liv drowned in the cold fear crippling her as that voice in her head became loud again. *You weren't enough for Gavin. You won't be enough for Miles. He'll resent you for making him move. He'll hate you for it. And you'll be left alone… again.*

THE NEXT MORNING, Miles woke to sun glistening through the sheer curtain. He'd left the patio door open last night, and the wind now made the fabric dance. Since he'd arrived on the cruise, he'd been dreading today. But after last night's call, he felt surer about his next steps than ever before. While he'd miss his family in Vegas, he didn't doubt himself now. He'd always lived by his mother's code: *work first, everything else second.*

That had only made him lonely. If he planned to risk it all, Liv was certainly worthy. He flipped over, expecting to find her sleeping.

Instead, he found a note on her empty pillow.

Dread sank in when he reached for the piece of paper.

What scares me more than losing myself, is being the reason that you lose who you are. Your friends need you. I refuse to be the reason you leave them and your job behind. I'll never forget this time we had together… I'll never forget you.

—Liv

"Fuck," Miles growled, shoving off the sheets. Obviously, she'd overheard the conversation last night between him, Dmitri, and Presley. A conversation that, on the outside, looked like he was giving everything up for *her*, but what she didn't realize was this decision was happening regardless of what happened on this cruise. He'd planned to make a move—maybe not forever and maybe not to San Fran—but at least until he found whatever he was looking for. Dmitri had known this. Presley hadn't.

But he'd found what he wanted in Liv. Something bigger than himself. Happiness.

He threw on a pair of pants and a T-shirt, not bothering with shoes. He snatched his wallet off the table and ran out the door. People were already packed and heading down the hallway with their suitcases. His heart raced, pulsing with dread as he pushed harder to get to her. Every second felt like a lifetime as he raced up the staircase then down another hallway until he reached Liv's cabin. He banged on the door. Again. And again.

Behind him, a soft voice said, "She's not in there."

Miles whirled around, finding Grace standing in her doorway, with Liv's other friend, Benjamin, there too. "Where is she?" he asked, breathless. "I need to find her." Because somehow, he knew if she left this ship that was it. She'd decide to walk away for good, to stop feeling and let logic win.

"I'm sorry, Miles," Grace said softly. "She's already left, and I suspect is on her way to the airport."

Benjamin cursed softly. "And obviously, she didn't tell you that." He slowly shook his head, a frown marring his face. "I feel for you, man. We've all got that look on our faces right now. Who knew a trip could end up with so many miserable people?" He turned and strode back into the room.

Grace stepped further into the hallway, leaving the door ajar. "I know I should probably stay out of it, but she cares about you, you know. Leaving you today…that wasn't easy for her."

Miles took in a shuddering breath, not having the words to explain what he felt right then. "Have a safe trip home." He turned away before he lashed out at a person who didn't deserve it. He wanted Liv with him, not lost in her fears, running back home.

He made it back to his cabin, cursing again as he slammed the door behind him. Just as he took a step forward, his cell phone rang. He snagged it from his pocket and answered the Facetime call before he even looked at the screen. Heady disappointment sank into him when he saw Cora.

"Miles, I'm just so happy for you and Liv," said Cora, a huge smile on her face. "Is she there? Am I interrupting? Oh, I just want to hear about your entire trip. Presley said it was amazing. I, for one, am so happy for you and that you're moving to San Fran. It'll give us even more reason to come visit. I love it there."

Miles wanted to curse. Why couldn't Liv have heard *this* conversation? Presley was sweet and loving and cared extra hard. His move would be hardest on her. But not hard on everyone. Liv simply didn't know that.

Whatever crossed his face made Cora frown. "Wait. What's wrong?"

Every fucking thing. "I need to go, Cora."

"What's happening?"

"I'll tell you when I come home."

Her eyes saddened. "You're coming home? To Vegas?"

"Yes." He ended the call. "Fuck," he growled, sitting

on the bed, thrusting his hand in his hair. He stared down at his phone, tension nearly crippling him, and then he opened that email that started all this.

Dear Miles,

Sometimes a connection doesn't make sense. It can hit us out of nowhere and change everything we know. I've thought about you every day for the past three months. If you have too, come cruise with me.
—Liv

The details of the cruise had been attached. Miles stared at the email now for as long as he'd stared at it after he received it. To go to Liv had been a decision he'd come to quickly. He thought fate had led him to the right spot.

Now fate only showed him a taste of what life with Liv could be, and then, like a cruel joke, that life was ripped away.

Miles shut his eyes, breathed deep, and then shoved his phone in his pocket, accepting the truth. He'd come to claim Liv as his. And he'd failed.

CHAPTER 12

THE NEXT MORNING, rain had descended on San Francisco. It matched Liv's mood perfectly. As she rode the elevator in the high-rise apartment building in the Soma neighborhood, soft music played and grinded on her nerves as she ascended to the 5th floor. On the cruise ship, she'd been so sure about her decision to leave Miles and come home. Alone. Now that she had woken up without him, nothing seemed right anymore. In fact, everything basically sucked. She questioned her decision to leave him a thousand times over, but kept coming to the same realization. Letting love happen was a choice. And while she felt like she'd left her heart on that cruise ship, she couldn't let Miles make such a huge choice for *her*. Fate couldn't dictate between right and wrong, and having Miles leave his found family all for something they had no idea was going to work, felt horribly wrong. And selfish. Although she knew she wanted him now more than ever, there was one thing she couldn't do: Be the reason he left those he loved behind. *And you're saving yourself from heartbreak.* Liv wanted to tell that voice to piss off.

Just as the doors chimed open, her cell phone rang. She reached for it in her purse. *Aubrey* showed on the screen. "Oh, my god, you're alive," Liv said by way of greeting.

Aubrey laughed. "Alive."

Liv exited the elevator, spotting her reflection in the large mirror on the wall. She quickly turned away, refusing to acknowledge the dark circles under her eyes. "I take it that means things haven't gone well with Carter?"

"I'll save you the long story, but let's just say things were great, then they're weren't, and it all ended with everything blowing up in my face."

"I'm so sorry."

"Me, too," Aubrey said, unusual sadness in her voice. "It's not like the logistics would have worked anyway, even if we'd tried."

Try. Liv hadn't even tried. She'd run. She swallowed the emotion climbing up her throat, as Aubrey asked, "And how about you and Miles? Anything come of that?"

"I left him on the ship."

A pause. A long pause. "And do you regret that?"

"Yes. No. Hell, I don't know."

When Aubrey spoke again, her voice softened. "Listen, Liv, I know dating again is scary. It is for anyone.

But every time I saw you on that cruise, you were lit up. I've never seen you like that. Not even when you were with Gavin. You need to stop letting that asshole, and what he did to you, control your life. You deserve a guy like Miles. One that makes you happy."

Liv's throat tightened further but she managed, "The sad thing is I thought Gavin wasn't controlling my life anymore. I know this is a mess and I've got to figure it all out, but I'm at my parents now and need to grab Fritz. Can I call you later?"

"I'm here. You know that. Love you."

"I do know that. Keep your chin up, Aubrey. Love you too."

"Thanks, babe. Bye."

Liv tucked her phone back into her purse then moved toward her parents' front door. They used to live in a cute two-story that was in all of Liv's happy childhood memories, but once Mom need the wheelchair, the condo made more sense.

Everything felt wrong and backward when she opened the door. She took a step in, saw her parents sitting on the couch, Mom's wheelchair next to her while she knitted. Her cute bob haircut was fresh, as was the brown color.

"Sweetie, you're home," Mom said, her blue eyes warming with her smile. "Your baby is waiting for you."

That baby, Fritz, the grumpy tabby cat, stood up,

meowed, and jumped off the couch to saunter over to her.

"I've got no doubt he's glad you're back," her father said, rising from his recliner in the corner. His salt and pepper hair looked like he'd also had a fresh cut recently, and his eyes, the same color as hers, looked mildly annoyed. He wrapped her in a warm hug and then smiled. "He hates us."

"Fritz hates everyone," Liv said. He stopped in front of her and tolerated a pet before flicking his tail and moving away to his food dish.

"Come sit down, tell us all about your trip," Mom said, patting the spot next to her on the couch. "Did you enjoy yourself?"

Liv wasn't sure if it was the loving tone her mother used, the sweet look on her face, or the question itself, but she suddenly burst into tears. All the emotion she had locked up tight overflowed with no stop button.

"Oh, dear," Mom said, concern on her face. "Harold, go get your daughter a glass of wine, she needs it."

That glass of wine, and the long talk with her mother, helped Liv focus on what she truly wanted. She left Fitz with her parents for a little while longer, and hurried down the busy street, the thick fog from earlier slowly dissipating. Her umbrella was not doing much to keep her dry, water splashing over her rain boots and soaking her tights. When she reached the high-rise that housed not only Allie's real estate company but also Holt Enterprises, Micah's multi-million-dollar corporate real estate company, she rushed into the lobby. She shook her umbrella out, blew the wet hair out of her face and then quickly made it onto the elevator and up to the 10th floor.

Allie's corner of this building looked nothing like Micah's masculine space with chrome and gray colors on just about everything. Allie's space, which included her corner office, a reception area, and Liv's office across from Allie's was warm and inviting, often reminding Liv of a beach house escape. While the walls were a pale beige, the accents were all warm blues.

Allie's office door was open. Liv went straight for it, keeping her thoughts focused on the reason she'd come. Knowing she'd lose her nerve if she didn't, she sputtered, "Allie, I love you, but I quit."

Behind her desk, Allie blinked. "Huh? Wait, you're not supposed to be here." She glanced at her watch then back at Liv. "Wait. You...*what?*"

"I quit," Liv said, gentler this time as she dropped down into the client chair. "Please don't say anything or I'll never get through this."

"Okay," Allie said with caution.

Liv took a deep breath and then began. "I have loved working for you. Honestly, it was more fun than I think I ever thought I'd have at a job, but I can't stay because I love you. When I went on the cruise, and spent those days with Miles, it's like I suddenly saw that I'm missing out on this big world that I've barely even seen. I'm not even sure when my dreams became unimportant, maybe after Gavin...who knows...but I need to start finding the things that make me happy. And once, going into corporate real estate had been my dream. I need to get back to that. So, that's what I'm going to do."

Softness reached Allie's eyes as she smiled. "Well, then I'd say that luck is on your side, because my husband owns the top corporate real estate company in San Francisco and I'm sure he would love to help you succeed."

Emotion clogged Liv's throat. She shouldn't have been surprised at Allie's love and support, but a part of her was. "Really?"

"Of course." Allie rose to come around her desk to wrap Liv in one of her amazing hugs. "Sure, you're the best assistant ever, but you're right, this is a big world, filled with lots of people. I can find someone who comes a close second."

Liv hugged Allie a bit harder now, finally feeling like she was on track toward making things right again. Since the cruise, nothing made sense anymore. It was like she'd left as one woman and come back another. She desperately wanted to reach out to Miles and tell him she'd just quit her job. She wanted to hear his voice. But where would that get them? She really didn't want to set her Facebook status to *complicated.*

That didn't stop her from missing him. Not just the sex either. She missed everything. The way he listened, that heat-packed smile, even his cool, calm nature. But the truth remained: Miles was in Vegas. Where he belonged. She couldn't change that, but her mother helped her realize, she could change her job. She could use what she discovered about herself on the cruise and do something with it. Grow from it. "Thank you for supporting me," she told Allie.

"Of course," Allie said, taking Liv's hands. "Whatever you need, both Micah and I are here for you. If you have forgotten, we really love you. A lot."

Liv squeezed Allie's hands in return. "I love you both too. Crazy hard."

"You know who else I think loves you?" Allie's eyes twinkled.

"Please don't say it," Liv said, pulling her hands away. "I'm trying to not to think about *him.*"

Allie cocked her head, sadness touching her eyes. "I really want to support you here, but Miles and you…it's a good thing."

"It is a good thing," Liv agreed. "But it's a complicated thing. How can I ask him to move here and leave all of his friends and his job? I can't take him away from his life in Vegas. It's just wrong." Liv drew in a big deep breath. "And beyond that, we both know who Miles is and the interests he has. Sure, we had fun this past week together, but I don't think I can be what he needs."

"Did you ask him what he wants?"

"He said he wants me."

Allie frowned. "But you don't think he's telling the truth?"

The answer was all too easy. "I feel like he *thinks* he knows what he wants, but when it comes down to the reality of it, he'll realize that I'm just this boring woman, not this wild woman he thinks I am."

Allie snorted. "My experiences with Doms is that they know exactly what they want. And if they don't, they go find it. Whatever he is saying to you, it's the truth, Liv."

She considered and shrugged. "Maybe, but I left. It's done."

"So that's it then? It's just over?"

"Yes," Liv said with a heavy sigh. "We had a thing. A great thing. But now I can get back to my life."

Allie's mouth twitched. "Sounds all very logical, but there's a big problem with that."

"Which is?"

"Emotions aren't logical."

Right then, there was a knock at Allie's door. "Hey, Allie, I know I'm a little early—"

Liv turned in her chair, meeting bright blue eyes that

once charmed her. Gavin had not changed one bit. Same suit. Same golden-brown stylish hair. Same gorgeous face and hot bod. All the things the ladies loved. A little too much.

Gavin stopped dead. "Liv."

"Hey," Liv said, and rose. Before the cruise, she wasn't sure how she would have felt if she'd run into Gavin. Because Allie was such a good agent, Gavin often would send his corporate clients to her when they needed a residential agent, and in turn Allie would send Gavin hers. Micah only dealt in multi-million-dollar deals so, unfortunately for Liv, the deal between Allie and Gavin still worked. But Allie had always done her best to get Liv out of the office if she and Gavin had to have a meeting. But now, as she faced the man who once crushed her, she didn't feel weak like she once had. If anything, she felt sorry for him. Sorry that he could have had anything he wanted but ruined everything he touched, and hurt those who cared about him. But most of all, she saw weakness compared to Miles. She turned to Allie and gave her a quick kiss. "Thanks again for everything. Can I call you guys later to talk to Micah?"

"I'll do one better," Allie said, rising from her chair. "Come for dinner tonight. We can talk then."

"Perfect. I'll bring the wine," Liv said, then turned to approach Gavin.

He followed her with his gaze as she closed in on

him, catching that citrusy cologne that she once thought was the best smell in the whole world. He gave her a full once-over. "You're looking good." He smiled.

At that, she smiled back. "Yeah, six days of wild, hot sex can do that to someone."

The shocked look on his face was decidedly her greatest revenge. She left a laughing Allie behind and stepped into an exciting future.

BACK IN VEGAS, late in the night, Miles headed down the strip, past the Bellagio fountains. The dancing water lit up and entertained the crowd gathered there, but Miles kept his focus on the glowing sign ahead: *Club Sin.* Bouncers contained the lineup of customers waiting to dance the night away in the nightclub, unbeknownst to them that there was an exclusive BDSM dungeon hidden in the back of the building.

"Miles," the bouncer, Jeremy, said as Miles reached the door. "Nice to have you back."

"Good to be back," Miles said, passing by to enter the club.

The nightclub was both classy and elegant. The flashing lights, the hundreds of people dancing; Miles was going to miss this place. But with or without Liv, change had to happen. Even as he walked through the doors, it felt like the wrong place to be. A place that would hold him back, instead of pushing him forward.

Chandeliers hung over the bar. Black leather couches were off to the side, and against the back wall behind the huge black glass bar was a glowing bright red sign: *Club Sin.* The place was busting at its seams, and Miles took pride in that. He'd only had full control of the nightclub for a year, and he'd succeeded in turning the bar into the best hotspot in the city, beating out many of the casino bars. And yet, being back in this space only reminded him that the fulfillment he craved when he sold his construction company was never found within these walls. He found that in Liv. And without her with him, nothing seemed right. He missed her.

He skipped the bar, moving quickly up the stairs to a roped-off VIP area. Another bouncer there gave Miles a nod and then opened the rope to allow him through. All the tables were full of partygoers enjoying bottle service. Miles headed past them, moving to the back door. He typed in a code and the door clicked open, giving him access to a dimly lit long hallway, until he stopped at a security guard.

Miles nodded at the guard. "Matthew."

"Good evening, Master Miles," Matthew replied, wearing the all black Club Sin uniform. He gestured to the little box near his keyboard. "Fingerprint, please."

Security was tight and strict, and even Miles wasn't

exempt from being identified. Logs were kept, nothing missed. He pressed his finger against the scanner. It beeped once.

Matthew studied the screen and then gave a firm nod. "Enjoy your night, sir."

"Thank you." The moment Miles cleared the next doorway, heat brushed across his flesh as energy hummed in the space. He scanned the large rectangular room, finding all the BDSM stations in use, and while the men were dressed in casual wear, the women wore classy lingerie.

Miles strode through the club, nodding at members who offered him a greeting or a smile. But soon, he found what he was looking for.

His friends. His family. And as odd as it was, it felt like someone was missing. Liv, she should be there too. At his side.

His close friends all sat in their usual spot in the center of the room, the best spot in the dungeon. Any station could be viewed from this spot, and all eyes were currently on the newest Dominant, Master Dylan, who had moved to Vegas recently from Salt Lake City. He had the submissive, Kelly, hogtied in suspension bondage. She was currently being near tormented with the vibrator Master Dylan controlled.

Home sweet home. And yet, as his friends caught sight of him, their frowns mirrored what Miles felt inside.

"While your tan is amazing and you look refreshed, you're also not supposed to be here alone," Cora said. "Where's Liv? And what the hell happened?"

"She went home," Miles said, taking a seat next to Cora, while she sat beside her husband, Aidan.

"Is there a reason for that?" Aidan asked.

Miles leaned back in his seat, crossing an ankle across his knee, taking in the sounds of pleasure filling the space. He glanced at Presley and Dmitri. "She overheard our conversation. Guilt of my leaving you all and Vegas had her fears rising and sent her running."

"Oh no," Presley said, covering her bulging breasts in her push up bra. "Was it something I said? I feel terrible. I didn't mean that I wasn't happy for you, just that I was really going to miss you. You know how I am, I get so emotional. Should I call her and explain?"

Miles shook his head, shutting that thought down immediately. "First, it's not something I did, or she did or anyone else did, but it's the nature of a wounded heart. She kept looking for a way out. She found one and took it."

Kyler reached out to stroke his wife Ella's, neck, as she sat on the armrest of his chair. "Is there nothing you can do?"

While Kelly's orgasmic scream filled the silence, Miles ran his hands over his face, admitting to his friends, "I did what I could do, but I failed at convincing her we're worth the risk. It *is* a wild thought. We've known each other for a week in total. What else can I do but offer to move to where she is?"

Porter frowned, and glanced at his wife, Kenzie, who said, "Well, if she's too stupid to see how amazing you are, then she doesn't deserve you anyway."

Always the outspoken one, Miles gave Kenzie a frown. "It is what it is," he said. "And she's not stupid, she's scared."

A long moment of silence passed. Master Dylan began untying a very satisfied Kelly, who was both panting and laughing simultaneously.

"All right, so what are you planning to do now?" Presley asked, drawing Miles' gaze again. "Does that mean you're going to stick around here with us?"

Miles leaned back in his seat and glanced out at Club Sin again. He took in the sounds of pleasure filling the space. The happiness there. The freedom this space gave to others, making them feel alive and sensual. "When I took over Club Sin," he said, addressing the whole group, "I was thrilled to not be working fourteen-hour days at a construction company. I thought I'd find something new that excited me and fulfilled me in between these walls."

"And did you find that?" Ella asked.

"I found all of you," he told them honestly. "I found close friends that have become a family I never knew even existed. I found that love can be healthy and good and real. I found that there is more to life than success and money." He glanced at Dmitri and admitted, "I learned that a love I didn't know existed is possible for me…and I finally found it."

"With her," Presley whispered.

Miles nodded. "With her."

Cora nibbled her lip. "Well, I think this is all very simple. You need to be your Dominant self and not take no for answer. So, how exactly are you going to do that?"

Miles gave the most honest answer of his life, and the most non-Dominant answer he had in him. "I have absolutely no fucking idea." And he didn't. He glanced out around him, knowing he could work any woman's body in this club until she was writhing in pleasure. But Liv's heart, he didn't know what to do with that. "Got any ideas?"

"Call her," Ella said.

"Fuck that," Kyler added. "Go to her. Fight for her."

"But where would that get him?" Cora asked. "In the same circle of her pain. You need to give her time. She'll come around."

Aidan agreed with a nod. "You've done the ground-work. If it's meant to be, it'll be."

Miles slowly shook his head and glanced at Presley. She shrugged. "I've already made a mess. I'm not saying anything more."

Dmitri cupped her chin, drawing her gaze to his. "You've done nothing wrong, doll. You just shared your feelings." He dropped a kiss on her lips then looked to Miles. "I suspect you're right. She was waiting for a reason to run and found it."

Kenzie chuckled. "I have no idea why she'd be scared. You're not intimidating at all."

Soft laughter filled the space around Miles. "Liv never met the Dominant. She had nothing to be intimated by."

Cora cocked her head. "But is that a good thing? Did she even get to know you?"

Miles considered that and rubbed his hands over his face again, feeling edgy. He wasn't even sure if he knew himself right now. And he didn't fucking like it. "Probably not." But somehow, he felt like she knew the parts that mattered. The parts that no one, except Miles's friends, knew.

Silence sank heavy between them. Until Porter broke it. "If you want something else to think about, I found out the building where that email was sent from."

At that, Miles's back went ramrod straight. "Tell me."

"Oh, now this is going to be fun," Kenzie said, bouncing in her seat. "Things are about to get really interesting."

CHAPTER 13

TWO WEEKS HAD flown by. Each day seeming a bit longer than the one before it. Liv felt as winded on this foggy night as she had the day she stepped on the cruise and saw Miles sitting there, and thought he was a figment of her imagination. She missed him terribly. Which only had her questioning her decision to leave him. Maybe she'd gotten this all wrong. All she wanted was some wine, a bath, and possibly a therapy session. But tonight, the glitz and the glam of San Francisco's elite surrounded her as she headed down the long hallway, wearing a gorgeous, black sparkly evening gown she'd borrowed from Allie's closet. Micah and Allie brought her to introduce her into Micah's very lucrative business world. "Maybe this was a mistake," Liv said to Allie, feeling out of her element as they entered the grand ballroom.

Allie rolled her eyes, linking her arm with Liv's. "Please. This is your night to network and meet people in Micah's world. You need an in, and this is your way to get it."

Of course, Allie was right. Liv had been playing it safe. She couldn't do that anymore. And that was one takeaway from Miles. She wanted to live like him. Going after her dreams, not hiding from them. Fears made her run. And that didn't make her feel good. Not one bit. She felt like a coward.

Determined to not waste this chance, Liv lifted her chin and strode into an unknown world where her dreams existed.

Three hours later, her cheeks hurt from smiling and her throat was dry from all the talking. With Micah and Allie chatting her up and introducing her to everyone, she had three job interviews lined up, with two of the agencies willing to pay for her to get her real estate license. Everything she ever hoped and wished for was happening. All her years with Allie had given her hands-on experience. And yet...*and yet,* the one person who encouraged her to make her dreams a reality wasn't here.

Miles.

He should be here.

Needing air and a minute to breathe, she made her way outside to the patio where people smoked cigarettes and cigars. She went on the other side of the balcony, staring out at the glowing lights on the Golden Gate Bridge, wondering if Miles was doing the same thing, staring out at the Vegas strip.

"Everything all right?"

She glanced over her shoulder, finding Micah. He looked like he strode out of GQ magazine in his tux and styled dark hair.

He offered her a glass of wine. "Thought you might need this," he said.

"Thanks." She smiled. "And yes, everything is perfect. I cannot thank you enough for helping me. You and Allie, you're both so special to me. I appreciate it all so much."

Micah slid his arms against the railing on the balcony, holding a glass of scotch between his hands. "Allie's business is successful, not only because of her, but because of you. We both know that, Liv. You deserve to thrive in the type of work you enjoy." At her answering smile, he added, "Which is why, even though you've got a few interviews lined up, I really hope you consider letting Holt interview you too."

She straightened up. "You want to interview me?"

"Of course, I'd love to have you on my team," he said, then leaned in closer and grinned. "But we'd only interview you for appearances and legality reasons. If you'd consider working for Holt, you've got the job. We'll get you in for your license next week and get that all squared away."

She waited for a man to pass by as he puffed on his cigar before addressing Micah again. "Why didn't you just ask before bringing me here tonight and helping me network?"

He took a long sip of his scotch, the ice clanging against the glass. "Why would I refuse you the right to choose? Now you've got my offer and you can see you've got options out there. But I hope you choose wisely and choose me." He laughed.

Liv nudged her shoulder into his, not sure what she did to deserve the friends she had, but she was glad for them. "You're too good to me, Micah. Both you and Allie."

"You're not giving yourself enough credit," he said, a softness in his voice she hadn't heard before. "You're a good friend to Allie, and you're a good person. You deserve to be happy, Liv." He glanced out at the twinkling lights, the side of his mouth curving. "Speaking of your happiness, did you ever find out who sent Miles that email?"

"Sadly, no." But now, instead of throttling them, she almost wanted to thank them. Her life had changed. And while her heart hurt, and she felt more confused than ever, the result of that email woke her up in more ways than one.

Micah took another sip of his drink and then he turned to her, leveling her with that steady gaze. "Must've been someone who cares about you very much and thought Miles would make you very happy."

The lightness of his gaze had her turning to him fully

then. *Did he…could he have noticed Liv's strong feelings for Miles?*

Micah stared out at the city lights. "You know, from what I've learned in life, fate has a hand in most things, but not everything. Sometimes it takes an idea and a little push. And sometimes all you've got to do is take a leap of faith, no matter how scary it might be."

Emotion made her throat tighten as she glanced down to the dark water below the bridge. A thousand thoughts crossed her mind, but one held steady. "You're right—whoever sent Miles that email had to be someone who cares about me. Had to have known that I did feel something for him that was magical. And if he lived here, he would have made me very happy. But that certainly proves my point that none of this is simply about taking a leap of faith."

Micah slowly cocked his head. "Then what is it about?"

She turned to him and sighed. "To have him, he'd have to give up everything. How is that fair?"

Micah polished off his scotch and shook his head. "Your fear has you thinking in absolutes. In black and white. There is a middle ground there. Miles is wealthy. That company of his, he sold that for millions, which I'm sure he never said because that's just not who Miles is as a man. Who's to say you can't go to Vegas once a month to visit his friends? Or travel there for weeks at a time for your vacations? Or have them come here? Or go on vacations somewhere with them? That's what love is. Sacrifice. You do whatever you've got to do to make it work, but you both have to work at it. As far as I can tell, Miles has done his part. Have you?"

The question was like a punch to the gut. Had she?

No. She'd been terrified. She'd put up roadblock after roadblock and Miles had expertly knocked down every one. She had kept waiting, looking for that thing that would crush her. The way Gavin had crushed her. And yet, Miles only helped her, not hurt her. If anything, she'd come out of their time together stronger, searching for her dreams to come true. But she hadn't been strong enough to do the one thing Miles deserved. Stay.

Suddenly, she knew. Miles wasn't Gavin. He'd never do what Gavin had done to her, and she believed that bone deep. "Shit," she gasped. "I made a big mistake, didn't I?"

Micah gave a firm nod. "Huge."

The world spun around her. Whatever hold Gavin still had, and all the damage he caused, finally broke away. "I shouldn't have left him."

"Nope," Micah agreed.

Her body flushed; her legs begged to run. To *him*. "How do I fix this?"

"An apology is a good start."

"Would an apology be enough?"

Micah gave a sly smile. "You're a smart woman, Liv. I've got no doubt in that clever mind of yours you can think up a pretty damn good apology that would make Miles unable to do anything but forgive you."

The answer hit her like a brick to the face. "Can you…would you…"

Micah grinned, and obviously, reading her mind, added, "I can. And yes, I will."

LIFE WOULD CHANGE after tonight. Change in ways that Miles knew would last forever. The last couple weeks had made him unravel. Something had to give. He'd tampered his dominating ways with Liv, controlled the side of him that liked to take control, both in the bedroom and out of it. That side made him successful, set him up financially to now be able to take time to figure out this new life he wanted. But the time to control that pulsating side of power stopped tonight. No, tonight Miles took all the things he wanted, all the things he needed. But first, in Club Sin's VIP area, Miles grabbed his phone and dialed the one person he'd waited to call until he cooled off.

Micah answered on the third ring. "I've been wondering when you were going to call me. My security indicated someone tried to get through our firewall. I'm guessing that was Porter."

"Indeed," Miles said, leaning back against the wall, staring out at the nightclub that would soon be packed full. "I knew my group here in Vegas would never cross those lines." The trust between them was too tight, but Miles only knew Micah through Dmitri. "Tell me why you sent the email and interfered with my life."

A pause. Then when Micah spoke again, emotion filled his voice. "For her."

"Because you love her?"

"Because she loves my wife and my wife loves her. Because she's a good woman, and a good friend to me. Because she never deserved the pain handed to her. Because when she met you at the wedding, there was something in her eyes I'd never seen before."

"What was that?"

"Hope."

Emotion slammed into Miles's chest. He wasn't quite sure what to say to Micah after Porter told him who'd sent the email. At first, he'd been furious. Now, things had changed. "Thank you, Micah. For the push."

A smile filled Micah's voice. "Take care of her."

The phone line went dead. Determined now to set the plan in motion that had finally all come together early this morning, Miles entered through the private door of Club Sin, knowing tonight would be his last time coming here for a while. This time, he kept his head down, quickly finding his group to say goodbye. "I've made a decision," he said, when he reached them.

All heads turned to his direction.

"Oh?" Dmitri said, with a topless Presley sitting on his lap.

"Kyler was right. I need to fight. I can't sit here and wait. My truck is packed. I'm hitting the road tonight for San Francisco. Liv might hate me for it, but damn if I won't fight like hell to keep her."

"Well, we all know I do give the best advice," Kyler said with a sly grin. "But I think you might want to rethink your plans to drive tonight." His grin widened as he gestured at something over Miles's shoulder.

Miles glanced back, and the world stopped turning. He grunted at the sheer force of emotion that hit him like a brick wall.

Low laughter came from behind him as Miles moved without even thinking, pulled forward in way he had never been before. He kept thinking his eyes were betraying him, but they weren't.

Liv stood on the stage, where nightly shows were done for the members by the Masters of Club Sin, Miles being one of them. His cock swiftly hardened at the strappy black lingerie set and black high heels she wore, and he groaned against the need flooding him. Her hair was up, leaving her neck exposed. Two leather cuffs were on her wrists. Miles's narrowed his eyes as he got closer. *His* cuffs. A black silk blindfold covered her eyes. *His* blindfold. Warmth hit him hard in the chest. His friends had arranged this, displaying Liv in all of Miles's favorite things.

He caught the way her head was tilted. She was listening. For *him.* And he spotted the way her mouth curved when he got close. He'd never had that before. A connection that went beyond a physical one, and he knew it was because he'd never met *her.* "You're here," he said, stepping up next to her.

"You're here," she whispered back.

Desperate to understand all this, he slid her blindfold off. "Yes, I am here. Why are you?"

She blinked once, adjusting to the light again. Those pretty eyes captured his. "I missed you."

"I missed you too," he told her, brushing his knuckles across her cheek.

Her eyes watered, lip quivered. "I'm sorry I left. What I feel for you…it's scary."

He arched an eyebrow, tightening his fingers, fighting against his desire to stroke her creamy flesh. "You're not scared anymore?"

"Deathly scared," she admitted. "But I'm tired of running, of being scared of what might happen. I want you, Miles. I want to see if we can make this work. Nothing was the same without you. I want this. I want *us*."

Elation burst through him, but that conversation of how they'd make this work would have to wait. He was about to show her his Dominant side. "Hmm," he murmured, feeling the energy in the room shift to him...to *them*. He stepped in closer, sliding his hand along her belly. "You should not have come here,"—her breath hitched, and he added before her mind could run away—"and offered yourself like this to me. You've stepped into *my* house, and this has changed the game."

She shivered and gestured to the right. "You can have me, Miles, in every way."

He caught sight of a piece of paper sitting on the spanking bench. One he'd seen many times before. He grabbed Club Sin's contract, along with a list of Liv's hard and soft limits and read it over carefully. All of her limits came as absolutely no surprise to him. They were the limits of a woman who wanted to be daring but feared anything extreme. All of which were perfectly fine with him. He'd done extreme. He wanted soft, sweet. He wanted her.

He set the paper down and moved back to Liv, catching her heavy breaths, full of nervous anticipation and excitement. "How did you arrange all this?" he asked, trying to understand how she got here.

"Micah contacted Dmitri," she said.

"He talked to Dmitri?"

She nodded.

Miles caught her chin. He lowered his voice. "Here. In this space. You'll respond with: Yes, Sir."

Her cheeks turned pink, glossy eyes held his. "Yes, Sir."

"Better," he said. He drew in a deep breath and took a step back to study her. Sure, this was his fucking dream come true, but he hesitated. The widened eyes, the rise and fall of her chest had him asking, "Help me understand your motives here. You're very nervous about being on display this openly, and yet, you're still doing it. Why?"

Her firm gaze held his, chin lifted, displaying the strength he loved in her. "I decided that I needed to level the playing field. If you're still all in, and willing to move to San Francisco for me, then I can do this for you when we're in Vegas. I want to be what you need. I trust you, Miles. I want to meet him."

"Who?"

"Master Miles."

Her sexy smile hit him like a heatwave. "If that's the case," he murmured, sliding the blindfold back into place, for no other reason than this would tease her. She liked having eyes on her. He wanted to play on that. "Let's have a little fun, shall we?"

She gasped when he took hold of the cuffs and led her forward. She followed in a way he wasn't expecting.

Total trust. She wasn't worried where her feet would land, she trusted he wouldn't let her fall. Damn, she was stunning. For years he'd seen his friends put their wives on display proudly, and now he understood. This connection, this show, it was special. Between just them in a way he'd never had before. Because this show wasn't for the crowd, this was all for them. His gift to Liv, and his salvation.

At the wooden board above her head, he *clinked* the cuffs into place. "Did you learn the club's safe word?"

"Dragon," she rasped.

He stroked along her back. "That's right, sweetheart. Use that word if things become too much." He stepped back, noticing a flogger waiting for him on the tray and a condom. And the moment he did, instrumental music filled the space. The soft, jazzy sounds that were his preference for playtime. At that, he glanced over his shoulder to his friends. All of whom were smiling at him. They'd gone to great lengths to ensure this moment with Liv was perfect.

Determined to take Liv to a place she'd never gone before, he grabbed the leather flogger from the tray and spun it in his hand, a heavy weight, the perfect extension of himself. This particular flogger gave more of a thudding hit than a painful bite, and the intention was to tease and excite, not drive a scene into mind-blowing intensity. No skilled Dominant would push a newbie, and Miles would not push Liv.

When he returned to her, he slid his hand down her back, loving the way she moved with his touch. He didn't waste time or pause to create nervous energy that would surely come. In the future, he'd love playing with those emotions. Building her up and up until she truly understood how intense pleasure freed a person. Now, he felt lost in the fact that she offered herself this way. The responsibility in that. The pride in it. He tucked the flogger under his arm to take hold of her panties and remove them. He unhooked her bra and nudged her legs open until she was spread wide, just how he liked her. Curious how she was reacting to this, he slid a hand across her belly then down to stroke her folds, finding her drenched in desire. "So fucking wet," he groaned. "So full of surprises."

"Yes, Sir," she gasped, rolling her hips with the strokes of his fingers.

He nipped her shoulder. "Good girl." Then he stepped back and began gently flicking the leather tails against her back, her bottom, until she was squirming under his touch. Her skin began turning red, her legs trembling slightly.

There was a time to push. Like, on the cruise, fighting for what he wanted. And there was a time to take what he needed.

Miles needed *her*.

When she began circling her hips with every hit on her bottom, showing him she'd been teased enough, he backed away. He opened his fly, took out his swollen cock and sheathed himself in the condom left for him on the tray. The crowd had gathered behind them, he could sense them there, watching. He quickly returned to her, flipped her around, spotting the color staining her cheeks. The redness of her lips telling him she'd been biting them. He kept the blindfold in place, nudged her thighs open again, and entered her, swiftly, right to the hilt.

She rose on her tip toes. "Holy shit."

He cupped her face, holding firmly, showing her just where she belonged. His other hand went to her hip. "I was going to come for you tonight," he told her. Even he heard the rough growl of his voice. "My truck was packed. I planned to fight for you."

She moaned.

He froze, pushed the blindfold off her face, met her glossy, lustfilled eyes. "I'll always fight for you, Liv."

"I'll always fight for you too."

His chest swelled with warmth as he grabbed her ass then gave it a firm swat. "Then there is really only one thing left to say isn't there? 'Master Miles, I am yours.' Let me hear that."

"Master Miles, I am yours," she breathed.

"Yeah, sweetheart, you are." He smiled, then he took

them where they both needed to go. The freedom, the release, the connection, as he left his one life behind and joined her in this new one.

CHAPTER 14

A COUPLE WEEKS had gone by since Liv left Miles in Vegas to come home, and those days felt long. Brutal. Life hadn't gone back to normal. If anything, Liv had never felt so alone.

"You look miserable," Allie said from the driver's seat of her Porsche sedan.

Liv glanced over and smiled. "Not miserable. Just hating the distance between me and the hottest sex of my life." Since her night at Club Sin, she and Miles had little time together. He needed to wrap things up in Vegas before moving to San Francisco, and the days had felt like forever. But she could wait. For *him.*

Allie laughed. "Yeah, that's got to be painful." She gave Liv a quick, understanding smile then glanced back on the road. "We won't be long, promise. Just want your opinion on this place."

Liv rolled her eyes. "Oh, yes, please take me back to the office because seeing all these dream houses is so terrible."

"Okay, yeah, I guess it's not a bad way to spend the

day," Allie agreed.

"I'm happy to be here with you," Liv said, then she studied the rows of houses with the manicured gardens. They were in the pricey waterfront central bay area in Foster City, only twenty-two miles from downtown San Francisco. Even if Liv saved everything she made for the next five years, she couldn't afford this neighborhood.

Allie slowed her car. "This town is a hidden secret," she said, pulling into the third driveway on the left and into a mid-century two-story red brick house. The gardens were well manicured, with mature trees scattering the property.

In quick time, they were walking up the stone pathway and made it inside. Liv gave a low whistle, taking it all in. "Wow, this place is incredible." Large windows brought in southern light, and a wood burning fireplace set in a stone was the highlight of the living room.

"Gorgeous right?" said Allie, shutting the door behind her. "It's got three bedrooms upstairs and two bathrooms."

"Not too big. Nice and cozy," Liv said, glancing up. "These high ceilings are amazing."

"Yeah, the entire floor plan is bright and open," Allie said.

And it was. Liv stepped into the middle of the living room with white oak engineered flooring, and she spotted quartz counters in the kitchen to the left. "I'm sold. When are you moving in?"

Allie laughed. "If you're in love already, wait until you see the backyard." She opened the patio door.

"Whoa," Liv purred, stepping out into a sunroom, which led to green grass that edged the water. She strode outside onto the grass and shielded her eyes from the sun as a pelican flew by. "Please, please, can you guys buy the place, so I can spend my weekends here?"

"It is really gorgeous," Allie said with a whimsical sigh.

A slow boat drove down the waterway, and Liv's cell phone beeped. She grabbed it from her purse, taking a quick look at the screen. "It's Micah," Liv reported. "He's got a property he wants me to take over. It's actually not far from here."

Allie gave a quick nod. "I'll drop you off. You can Uber back to the office later and expense it to Micah."

Liv laughed, turning away. "I'm sure he'll love that."

"Wait," Allie gasped. "So, what's the verdict on this place? Yes or no?"

Liv glanced around, green with envy. "A giant yes!"

"Good." Allie beamed. "Sold."

Liv was still a little jealous during the quick drive over to the address Micah sent her. But that ended when Allie pulled the car into the driveaway. Liv frowned. "Oh, no, they don't." The building had a few shops, but at the very end was San Francisco's animal shelter. Liv had been there, many times, to bring food whenever she had a little extra cash. "We are so *not* selling this property. Micah should know better than to give me this deal."

Allie shrugged. "You take it up with him. I'm staying out of it."

"Don't you worry, I plan to." Liv got out of the car and smiled at Allie. "Thanks for the break. I'll call you later."

Allie smiled in return. "Yup, I've got no doubt you will. See you."

Liv slammed the car door shut and then moved toward the building, hoping to hell they had a plan in place for a better location, maybe a bigger one.

The second she walked in, she stopped dead, wondering if she was having another figment of her imagination moment. She hadn't been having those lately, but maybe something in her psyche had gone wonky. She strode forward and poked a very hard chest. "Shit." She gasped. "You're real."

Miles barked a laugh. "Still doing that, huh?"

Liv blinked. Twice. "I don't understand what's happening. Why are you here?"

"Yeah, well, that winded, confused feeling is how I felt the day I met you," he said, taking her hand and bring her up against the strong lines of his body. "Makes us even now." Goosebumps prickled across her arms as he tucked her hair behind her ear, his soft gaze roaming over her face. "There was life before you, Liv. And life after you. I refuse to ever go back. We belong together. Now and forever." He dropped to one knee and opened a little black box. "Liv, will you marry me?"

Her breath caught at the gorgeous, brilliant-cut princess ring. "What's happening?" she managed.

"Well, I've just proposed marriage," he said, looking up at her with a sly grin. "And I'm waiting for you to say yes."

She blinked. "But you don't live here."

"I do now," he said. "My offer was just accepted on the house that Allie took you to see, which, if you're still in agreement, will be *ours*."

"Wait," Liv said, trying to catch up, the world spinning around her so fast. "Allie tricked me?"

"A little." He winked. "But all for a very good reason. And I know this is important to you, so you should also know I've accepted an architect position within a division at Holt."

"But you gave up construction?"

"No," he corrected. "I sold my specialized industrial construction company to have a personal life since I worked more than I slept. Architecture is what I went to school for. I'm excited to get back to my roots and get back to design." He paused to take a deep breath. "Now, I know you feel bad about having me move to San

Francisco, so here's the thing, Liv. I'm moving here for me, so you can stop feeling guilty about that." He gestured to the ring. "But I really want there to be an us. What do you say? Forever sound about good to you?"

A half laugh, half sob bubbled up and she lunged herself at him, feeling like the world suddenly made total sense. Fate had been right all along. All she had to do was believe in it…in herself…and in Miles. And she did. "Yes, I'll marry you. A thousand times yes."

His smile healed any remaining painful spots on her soul. Then he slid the ring on her finger and kissed her. Perfectly. Warmly. Everything she needed in this moment and so much more. "Now, since hitting the ground running is our thing, I vote for us to go right ahead and start a family."

She began leaning away. "Whoa, hold up—"

He burst out laughing. "Remember where you are. I'm not talking about children."

To remind herself, she glanced around, taking in the musky scent, seeing the dirty paw prints on the floor. She turned back to Miles with a gasp. "Are you talking about a puppy?"

He nudged her out of his lap and then rose. "You're working nine to five now. I plan to work those same hours once I start my job out here. They've got a great doggy daycare nearby. We've got the property. So, what do you say?"

The door suddenly opened, and six dogs ran into the room. She glanced back at Miles. "I say that you don't know what you're getting yourself into. There is absolutely no way I'm leaving with just one."

Miles gave her a tender kiss as puppies jumped up on her legs. "As long as I'm leaving with you, too, I'm happy."

EPILOGUE

Two years later…

SWEET BLUE EYES stared up at Liv as she finished buttoning up the onesie with the cute Koala's on the feet. "Keep looking at me like that, Luca, and I'll never be able to say no to you." She kissed his little nose and then swaddled him back up in the blanket. "Come on, my little buddy, everyone's waiting on you downstairs."

"Not only waiting on Luca." Liv glanced toward the door, finding Miles leaning against the doorframe, arms crossed. "They're waiting for my beautiful wife too."

"Okay, you better stop," Liv said with a smile. "If I get any happier, you might actually make me explode."

He chuckled and met her halfway, dropping a soft kiss on her mouth. "If you explode from happiness then I'll die happy, right alongside you." He leaned away to place a gentle kiss on Luca's head. "Get ready, my boy, you've got a room full of women who want to love you." He slid Luca onto his arm like a football and took Liv's hand.

They left the nursery, which had been Miles's home

office for the first year of their marriage and headed down the staircase.

The voices coming from the backyard hit Liv before they even made it out onto the patio. She got one foot out the door and spotted her father standing next to her mother, who sipped her wine in her wheelchair. Then her gaze fell to Aubrey, Benjamin, Grace, and Kendall, all with their significant others, when suddenly there were squeals of happiness and a rush of women overwhelmed her.

"Oh, my goodness, we flipped a coin, I get to hold him first," Presley said, scooping Luca up from Miles's arms.

Miles laughed softly. "I'm surprised you're all being so civilized and taking turns."

Cora rolled her eyes at Miles. "Of course we're being civilized. We're not going to maul your baby."

Kenzie grabbed a wine glass off the tray and snorted. "Don't believe a word she says. Before the coin toss, I swore there might be some hair pulling." She nudged Liv's arm with hers. "And not the good kind of hair pulling either."

"Lies," Presley cooed at Luca. "All lies. You sweet baby. Oh, my goodness, he's so alert."

"I swear he came out like that," Liv said. "But he also sleeps seven hours at night."

"Yes, you're lucky," said Allie, striding out the back

door with a bottle of red wine. She kissed Liv on the cheek and said to Presley, "Damion slept three hours tops as a newborn." Damion was Allie and Micah's six-month-old, who was currently bouncing in his father's arms as he came through the back door. Damion belonged on a baby food jar label with his dark hair and big, bright blue eyes.

"Well, enjoy the quiet as long as you've got it," Ella said, with a soft smile. "I had one just like this. All quiet and sweet." She pointed to her five-year-old running around the yard, along with Dmitri and Presley's two little children, chasing Romeo and Juliet, Liv and Miles's yellow Labrador Retrievers. "Now look at him."

Liv laughed. Maybe a little bit harder as Ella suddenly took off running after him when he began chasing after a bird, heading toward the waterfront. Her husband, Kyler, got there first, scooping their son up sending him squealing in laughter.

It was a good life. One Liv wasn't sure she'd ever have, but one that she felt blessed had become hers. All the fears she'd had that they couldn't make this work were for nothing. Miles saw his friends often. They came out to San Francisco, as much as Liv and Miles went out to visit Las Vegas…and Club Sin.

Warmth surrounded her as Miles sidled up to her, offering her some fruity cocktail. She took a sip. "Yum. Who made this?"

"I did," he said.

She took a better look at it, the drink had three different colors. "I didn't even know you knew how to make cocktails. Even after two years, you're still surprising me."

"Don't be too impressed. I actually don't know how to make cocktails." He gestured to the drink. "You don't remember that specific drink?"

She took another sip. "Nope. Should I?"

"That's the drink you ordered when I first saw you on the cruise."

"It is not?"

He nodded and smiled.

She glanced back at the drink, remembering that first night on the cruise when she thought Miles was a figment of her imagination. "Oh, my god, you're right. I ordered a Miami Vice. How did you remember that?"

"Don't you know what today is?"

The answer hit her. "Today is the two-year anniversary of the cruise, isn't it?"

He slid an arm around her, bringing her in close, and brushed his knuckles across her cheek. "Any regrets about staying on that cruise with me?"

She glanced out at her parents, watched as Presley handed off Luca to a smiling Aubrey, with Carter next to her, and all of their other friends circling around them. She smiled at Miles. "Not a single one." She angled her chin, standing up on her tiptoes. "I love you, Miles, and the life we have."

"My heart is now, and is always, yours, Liv."

About the Author

Stacey Kennedy is a *USA Today* bestselling author who writes contemporary romances full of heat, heart, and happily ever afters. With over 50 titles published, her books have hit Amazon, B&N, and Apple Books bestseller lists.

Stacey lives with her husband and two children in southwestern Ontario—in a city that's just as charming as any of the small towns she creates. Most days, you'll find her enjoying the outdoors with her family or venturing into the forest with her horse, Priya. Stacey's just as happy curled up indoors, where she writes surrounded by her lazy dogs. She believes that sexy books about hot cowboys or alpha heroes can fix any bad day. But wine and chocolate help too.

Stacey absolutely loves to hear from her readers. You can reach her at stacey@staceykennedy.com.

Connect with Stacey:
www.staceykennedy.com
Twitter @Stacey_Kennedy
Facebook.com/authorstaceykennedy

DON'T MISS A NEW RELEASE OR SALE!
SUBSCRIBE TO STACEY'S MAILING LIST:
www.staceykennedy.com/newsletter

Acknowledgments

To my husband, my children, family, friends, and bestie. It's easy to write about love when there is so much love around me. Big thanks to my readers for your friendship and your support; my editor, Lexi, for believing in me and making my stories shine; my agent, Jessica, for always having my back; the kick-ass authors in my sprint group for their endless advice and support; Priscillia Bernier for the French translations; Karen Roma and Peggy Lee, for sharing their cruise experiences which helped shape this story. Thank you.

Wonder what Kendall is getting up to? Read on for an excerpt from New York Times bestselling author, Katee Robert's:

KISSING KENDALL

CHAPTER 1

KENDALL BARNES REALIZED she'd made a terrible mistake the second she saw the pseudo-orgy going on by the pool. Did it even count as an orgy if they still had their clothes on and the ship hadn't left New York? She wasn't sure, but her face flamed at the way the group of five—*five?*—people surged and rolled as they made out and ground on each other. She couldn't be sure, but she was pretty sure that guy had his hand down that girl's pants and—

She turned away.

This was wrong.

This was very, very wrong.

"Kendall, those people are—"

"I know," she grabbed Grace and steered her away from the scene behind them. She'd known booking this cruise was a risk. Everyone knew cruises were a risk, what with so many people sandwiched in a relatively small space. But Kendall had been prepared to battle norovirus or seasickness or pirates. She was *not* prepared to deal with people getting to third base right there on the deck.

They hadn't even left port yet!

Their other three friends had already had their rooms assigned, but she and Grace were left to wander a little bit before theirs were ready. She looked around and finally landed on one of the cruise employees in their official-looking white uniform. "We'll just report them."

"*Report* them?"

She didn't give Grace a chance to argue, towing her along and dodging people streaming onto the ship. The guy in white gave them a professional smile as they approached, his dark skin gleaming in the bright sunlight. "How can I help you?"

Kendall made a vague motion over her shoulder. "Those people…"

The man leaned a little and smiled. "They're getting the party started early, it seems."

"Party?" She cleared her throat, well aware that her skin had to be crimson at this point judging by the heat in her cheeks. "Don't you think it's a little inappropriate for them to be… fornicating… on the deck when this is supposed to be a nice relaxing cruise?"

His dark brows rose. "Ma'am, that is the *least* of what you'll see over the next eight days on the party cruise."

Did he just…

He did.

She didn't realize she was tightening her grip on Grace's arm until her friend grabbed Kendall's wrist and forced her to let go. Kendall cleared her throat again, striving for calm that she could feel slipping through her fingers. "I'm sorry, I thought you said party cruise, but that can't possibly be right because I booked a *low-key relaxing cruise.*"

His smile went sympathetic. "One of your friends put this together, right? They must have thought it would be a great surprise. That happens from time to time."

She heard his words, but they still made no sense. Kendall didn't make mistakes. When she put together the perfect plan to reconnect with her old college friends, she'd worked with a travel agent to organize it down to the smallest detail. She had very specifically *not* booked a party cruise. She was not the kind of person who booked a party cruise. If anyone, that was her little sister's thing. In fact, she was pretty sure Marley went on one last year.

She shook her head. "There's been a mistake."

"Kendall."

She turned to look at Grace. Her friend didn't look like she was seconds from the panic attack Kendall could feel bubbling up in her chest. Grace's dark eyes narrowed and she took Kendall's shoulders. "Breathe."

"I am breathing."

"You're two seconds from freaking out."

She wasn't wrong. Kendall closed her eyes and concentrated on breathing. Without the sight of the orgy-in-waiting, she could almost pretend they were on the right cruise. Almost. "We have to get off this boat."

"Kendall, that's impossible."

She opened her eyes. "Nothing's impossible. You just have to speak to the right people."

Grace sighed. "Let's walk through it logically. Even if we could get to the others in time and convince them to leave the ship, our trip is paid for. We've all taken this exact block of time off work. We're *here*. The only thing that makes sense is to continue the vacation as planned."

As planned. Two little words to underscore how thoroughly she'd messed up. Kendall wrapped her arms around herself and tried to ignore pressure building in her chest. "I'm sorry. I'm so sorry. The whole trip is ruined."

"The trip hasn't even started yet," Grace's wry tone snapped her out of it.

What was she thinking? This couldn't possibly be worse than any other disaster she'd successfully navigated. She just needed to find the right angle and drag the rest of them along with her. Yes, she couldn't have possibly anticipated a *party* cruise in place of the nice sedate one planned, but she hadn't anticipated that her boss would run off with the front desk manager last year, either. She'd handled that crisis, and she'd handle this one too.

Simple.

This time, when she inhaled, it didn't snag in her chest. "You're right."

"I know."

Kendall managed a smile. "Let's get our rooms situated and then we'll figure out the rest."

"Figure out the rest," Grace repeated, giving her a look like she was a tiger in a cage. "You know you're on vacation, correct?"

"You're one to talk." She didn't comment on Grace's aversion to vacation wear, which really translated into an aversion to wearing *shorts*. It didn't make much difference now, while it was still cold and windy and they were too far north for anything resembling *warm*, but Grace wouldn't change her mind once the sticky heat set in. She'd just suffer in silence as if that made any kind of sense. Then again, they all had their quirks. "The only reason you agreed to this is because your CEO forced you to."

Grace opened her mouth, seemed to reconsider, and closed it. "Let's find our rooms."

"Checkmate." Kendall laughed, but it came out half-hearted. One of the cruise people called Grace's name and she waved her off. "Go get your room and warm up. I'll see you in a little bit when we meet for drinks." She *needed* a drink after this spectacular failure. She managed to keep her smile in place until Grace disappeared into the crowd, and then Kendall let her shoulders slump.

She should have known this would go sideways before the cruise ship even departed. If there was one law she ascribed to above all others, it was Murphy's. Anything that could go wrong, did. Every. Single. Time. It started with the death of her parents when she was nine, and it hadn't let up in the sixteen years since. Not once. She'd thought this trip would be the exception, the turning point she so desperately needed.

She really should have known better.

A sensation swept over her, stalling her before she could start pacing. Someone was watching her, their attention a weight she could feel as surely as she felt the cold nipping at her skin. She looked around slowly, telling herself this was silly even as she did. It didn't matter if someone was watching her. This was a freaking singles party cruise; no doubt people would look at her and assume she wanted in on the activities. They'd be wrong, of course. Kendall didn't do wild, and she sure as hell didn't hook up. With her long-running bad luck, it'd end even worse than her handful of relationships had over the years. She shuddered at the thought.

Her shudder turned into something else altogether when she met blue eyes across the deck. The man they belonged to leaned against the railing, looking particularly unaffected in his weathered jeans and leather jacket. His dark hair barely ruffled in the wind, and his square jaw looked sharp enough to cut herself on.

She turned her back to him immediately. Nearly two decades of crappy luck was enough for her to develop keen instincts when something would cause her an untold amount of trouble. Like every time her little sister said "I have a great idea," or whenever the owner of the hotel she worked for smiled and said "I know you have this covered."

Whoever that man was, he was trouble with a capital "T."

She wanted nothing to do with it—or him.

ALEX JEFFRIES WATCHED the little brunette scurry across the deck away from him. Everyone else waiting for their rooms seemed intent on starting the party early, despite the fact that the wind chill made the mid-March day feel like spring would never come.

He fucking hated New York.

Almost as much as he hated cruises.

Even though he knew better, he tracked the brunette's movements as she all but rushed to the harried looking cruise employee, no doubt to demand her room to get her away from the rest of the rabble. That one had high maintenance written all over her, from her pretty floral dress to her black tights and boots and the jacket that couldn't possibly hold up against this cold. She was the kind of person who dressed for visual appeal instead of function, and he'd met more than his fair share of *those* over the years.

"See something you like?"

"No." He reluctantly dragged his gaze away from her to look at Lucas. The only reason he was on this godforsaken cruise in the first place. It wasn't strictly true—Pop bought the tickets and all but strong-armed them both into coming—but if Lucas had made some excuse not to come, Alex could have gotten out of it. He *should* have gotten out of it.

Even though he knew, rationally, that his bar, Pop's, was in good hands for the next nine days, he couldn't shake the feeling that he'd arrive back in town to find it burned to the ground. That if he wasn't there every single day, putting in the time and effort, it would fall to pieces.

"You sure?" Lucas grinned. "Pop gave me clear instructions to make sure you had a good time."

"I know how to have a good time." *Too* good a time. Though if he was honest, it'd been a few years since that was true. He'd packed enough living—and mistakes—into his teens and early twenties to double the gray hairs on Pop's head, and after the old man's heart attack when Alex was twenty-two, he'd resolved not to be the cause of any more stress or worry.

That plan had backfired, though, because now Pop

was convinced Alex would die grizzled and alone in the bar the old man opened. It didn't sound like such a terrible fate from where Alex stood, but telling Pop as much had resulted in these fucking cruise plans. The grandfather he'd grown up with hadn't known the meaning of vacation, but apparently Mexico was enough to loosen some of those rules, and he expected Alex to fall in line, just like always.

It was only eight days. He could survive eight days of this bullshit.

"You're right. You know how to have a good time. That's why you're scowling at everyone." Lucas sighed. "Look, man, you don't have to party on this ship if you don't want to. *I* don't plan on it. But no reason not to enjoy yourself while you're here."

Easy enough for Lucas to say. He'd always been the even-keeled friend. The one who didn't have to make a conscious effort not to fuck up every single second of every single day. The most scandalous thing about him, if it could even be called that, was that he was bi and sort of in the closet about it, but that barely counted as a "problem." When Alex fucked up, he *fucked up*, and other people paid the price.

Better to avoid all that bullshit in the first place.

Lucas sighed. "I'm not saying go full party animal. Just smile for once instead of scowling. You're going to scare someone."

Someone like the little brunette who'd all but sprinted in the opposite direction the second she laid eyes on him. He couldn't tell the color of the eyes in question, but she had the most decadent lips he'd ever seen. Pouty and plump enough to have a man thinking sinful thoughts.

If that man was interested in getting into trouble.

Alex wasn't. End of story. But as he looked at his friend, he decided maybe Lucas was right. No matter that he'd been steamrolled into his vacation, there wasn't a single damn reason not to enjoy it now that he was here. The wind chose that moment to kick up, and he shivered. "Let's get this room shit sorted and get a drink."

"There he is." Lucas clapped him on the shoulder. "Trust me. This doesn't have to be a torturous experience. You might even have fun despite yourself."

"You should take your own advice while we're here."

Lucas grinned. "Maybe I will."

An hour later, their shit in their respective cabins and drinks in their hands, they stood by the bar that shone in the low light. It was as far from *his* bar as something could be and still maintain the same label. There were no scuff marks, no stains, no *character*. Everything was streamlined and perfect and left him feeling like the only flaw in the room was his shitty attitude. He could admit, at least to himself, that this might be exactly the change of pace both Lucas and Pop claimed he needed.

They'd barely left port, but the party was already in full swing. Despite the low music, a handful of couples writhed together next to the bar, a version of foreplay he'd seen played out with college kids countless times. They were young, well on their way to being drunk, and determined to live their lives to the fullest.

He seriously hoped this ship had stocked up on condoms, or they ran the risk of a widespread STD outbreak. The thought made him turn away from the scene. Fuck, he when did he get so *old?*

And there she was.

The brunette.

She stood around a tall table with three other white women and a guy, but she was the only one he could focus on. Her dark hair shone like some kind of beacon, the sight a hook in his chest. He actually took a step toward her before he caught himself. That shit was *not* why he was here. She might be pretty in the flawless kind of way that a perverse part of him wanted to smudge, but everything from her floral dress to her pretty pale pink lipstick was a giant neon warning sign for him to stay the fuck away.

That, and the fact she all but ran from him earlier.

Alex might be a dick sometimes, but he could take a hint. He forced himself to turn back to the bar. "I think I'm going to crash early."

"Nope." Lucas shook his head. "You're going to have fun, even if I have to drag your ass around behind me."

He snorted. "Pretty sure it doesn't count as fun if you're dragging me anywhere."

"The end result is all that matters."

Hard to argue with that, and he'd been friends Lucas long enough to know better than to try. The man hadn't taken them to state in high school and leveraged a successful college football career into a full-time coaching gig because he was a pushover. When he decided he was going to do something, he did it. Which was probably why Pop had sent him with Alex on this vacation. If anyone could ensure Alex got out of his own head, it was Lucas.

Maybe they were both right. It was only eight days in the grand scheme of things. He couldn't do a damn thing now. The ship had literally sailed. Either he could bitch and moan and be the asshole that ruined Lucas's vacation, or he could try to relax a little and try to enjoy it.

Try being the operative word.

Alex managed a smile. "Does this mean you want to do shots?"

"Fuck no, man. We're too old for that shit."

His grin widened. Nothing like a little payback to brighten his day. "Shots it is!"

In the Phoenix club, there is only one rule; watch, don't touch, until the powerful owner falls for his new star in this deliciously intriguing romance from *USA Today* bestselling author Stacey Kennedy.

Check out the first book in Stacey Kennedy's
Phoenix series. . .

WATCH ME

In one night, Olivia Watts' life goes from ordinary to out of this world after she's introduced to Rhys Harrington, the owner of Phoenix, an ultra-exclusive, upscale sex club. He's the one man she should stay away from… and the only man she wants.

Rhys needs a new performer for his high-end clients, who pay extravagant amounts to watch others indulge their fantasies, and one look at Olivia tells Rhys he's found his star. Only Rhys wants her all to himself, and the addictive passion between them sets the stage for the perfect show…

It'll be Olivia's choice to play Rhys's game. But if she says yes, there will be more on the line than just her pleasure. Because Rhys's sizzling touch doesn't only capture her body, it also commands her heart.

Find out more about *WATCH ME*.
Stay up-to-date with Stacey's new releases and join the mailing list HERE.
staceykennedy.com/newsletter

www.ingramcontent.com/pod-product-compliance
Lightning Source LLC
Chambersburg PA
CBHW032121170626
46808CB00006B/2046